About the Author

Frank Billingsley, with more than thirty years of experience across higher education, social services, secondary education, and business, brings diverse expertise to the debut novel, *His Love Has Two Sides*. As an accomplished academic, he has made notable contributions to esteemed journals and has presented at prestigious international conferences, highlighting his fervor for storytelling and captivating narratives. Holding a doctorate and three master's degrees in leadership, psychology, and environmental science, Frank's multifaceted educational background enriches the depth and authenticity of his literary endeavors.

His Love Has Two Sides

Frank Billingsley

His Love Has Two Sides

Olympia Publishers
London

www.olympiapublishers.com
OLYMPIA PAPERBACK EDITION

Copyright © Frank Billingsley 2025

The right of Frank Billingsley to be identified as author of
this work has been asserted in accordance with sections 77 and 78 of
the Copyright, Designs and Patents Act 1988.

All Rights Reserved

No reproduction, copy or transmission of this publication
may be made without written permission.
No paragraph of this publication may be reproduced,
copied or transmitted save with the written permission of the publisher,
or in accordance with the provisions
of the Copyright Act 1956 (as amended).

Any person who commits any unauthorised act in relation to
this publication may be liable to criminal
prosecution and civil claims for damage.

A CIP catalogue record for this title is
available from the British Library.

ISBN: 978-1-83543-318-8

This is a work of fiction.
Names, characters, places and incidents originate from the writer's
imagination. Any resemblance to actual persons, living or dead, is
purely coincidental.

First Published in 2025

Olympia Publishers
Tallis House
2 Tallis Street
London
EC4Y 0AB

Printed in Great Britain

Character Preface:

Nicholas Jameson (28 years old): A (discovering perhaps closeted) bisexual man, married to a woman, struggling with his identity and desires. Human Rights Lawyer.

Marc Anders (24 years old): An openly gay and confident young man, comfortable with his sexuality. New Graduate Library Associate. Blond hair. Blue eyes.

Wife Brooke: 28 Marketing Design: She possesses a graceful and timeless beauty that radiates from both her appearance and her demeanor. Blond bobbed hair, blue eyes.

Sam (24) Social Worker: appearance is a celebration of their authentic self, reflecting their gender identity with confidence and pride.

Chapter 1

Chance Encounter

The soft chime of the café's bell danced in the air, welcoming each newcomer into the cozy haven. On that seemingly ordinary morning, little did anyone know, it marked the arrival of an encounter that would kickstart a ripple of change in Nicholas' life. Nestled at a corner table, he had slipped into the café's embrace, seeking refuge from the predictable rhythm of his daily grind.

Nicholas fiddled with his coffee cup, the gleam of his wedding band catching glints of light as he absently traced patterns on the surface. His focus wavered between the swirls of steam from his coffee and the lively panorama outside the window.

Pedestrians hustled and bustled, a symphony of diverse stories blending into the city's fabric. It was a bustling tapestry that, despite its chaos, offered him a strange sense of solace.

Yet, even as he watched the world outside, his mind ventured deeper, wandering down the lanes of his own life. The loyalty he had pledged through that ring on his finger felt like a double-edged sword. Nicholas' fingers involuntarily traced the curve of the wedding band—an emblem of vows exchanged not long ago. Yet lately, it clung to his finger like a weight, a reminder of gaps and uncertainties that his thoughts danced around, unable to pinpoint.

The café's atmosphere cocooned Nicholas in a moment of introspection. With each sip of his coffee, he tasted the complexities of his thoughts—a concoction of loyalty, yearning, and questions about his path. As the city's rhythm continued its relentless beat outside, within that coffee-scented refuge, Nicholas' contemplations began to take on a life of their own, primed to intertwine with the chance meeting that was about to unfold.

Just as Nicholas was about to retreat further into his thoughts, the door chimed once again, its sound accompanied by a rush of chilly air. He glanced up, expecting nothing more than another stranger passing through the threshold. Yet, what he saw was a young man with a lively energy that seemed to radiate from him like a 'halo.' A tall, slender young man, with straight blond hair that framed and fluttered around his face as he looked left to right, noticing the lively atmosphere of the café. Nicholas was bemused by his confidence and style.

Nicholas' curiosity was piqued as he observed the stranger's entrance. The way the young man's blond hair framed his face and moved with every motion gave him an almost ethereal quality. It was as if he brought a burst of life and energy into the room, a stark contrast to the subdued thoughts that had occupied Nicholas' mind just moments earlier.

As the young man took in the café's surroundings with an enthusiastic gaze, Nicholas couldn't help but feel a mixture of surprise and admiration. There was something magnetic about the stranger's presence—a certain charisma that drew the eyes of those around him. The confident aura he exuded seemed to create an energy that enveloped him, setting him apart from the ordinary.

Nicholas found himself intrigued by the stranger's style and the way he seemed to effortlessly command attention. It was as if this guy had a unique ability to capture the essence of the moment and infuse it with his own effervescent spirit. His arrival brought a new dimension to the café, transforming it from a space of introspection to one filled with the potential for unexpected encounters and connections.

He seemed to hesitate at the door, momentarily scanning the room before his gaze settled on Nicholas. Their eyes locked in a moment that was all too fleeting yet somehow momentous. Nicholas' heart raced, caught off guard by the intensity of interest he felt for this intriguing guy. He soon disappeared around the corner, and Nicholas returned to his prior thoughts of life's discontent.

As Nicholas stared out the window, he heard, 'Do you mind if I join you? There are no other seats, and I really need a break.' Nicholas was suddenly forced back to reality.

'Um, yes,' Nicholas replied, his surprise at the steadiness of his own voice concealed beneath a veneer of calm. He cleared his throat, momentarily battling the unexpected flutter in his chest. 'I mean, please have a seat.'

The guy's smile widened, and the tension in the air seemed to ease a fraction. He took a deep breath, as if gathering his courage, before settling comfortably into the chair. The proximity between them was suddenly charged, an energy that Nicholas had never quite experienced before.

'Thank you for letting me join you; I needed a coffee. Hello, I'm Marc, Marc Anders, And you?'

Nicholas' facial expression turned slightly guarded, his brows furrowing as he processed Marc's openness. He took a moment to collect his thoughts and then directly addressed the situation. Or should he? Should he consider this to be odd or friendly? He was unsure; maybe he was reading more into this situation than intended.

He cleared his throat; his voice tinged with a touch of caution. 'Marc, ahem, hello, ahem, I'm Nicholas.'

Marc's eyes softened, understanding Nicholas' hesitation. 'I apologize if I overstepped. I'm always a little too forward.'

Nicholas took in Marc's response, his uncertainty momentarily mirrored in his gaze. He appreciated Marc's awareness and willingness to backtrack a bit. As he looked into Marc's eyes, he sensed a genuine kindness—an earnest attempt to bridge a connection rather than cause discomfort. The tension that had briefly settled in Nicholas' shoulders began to ease.

A small smile tugged at the corners of Nicholas' lips, his guarded expression giving way to a more relaxed demeanor.

'No need to apologize,' he replied, his voice gentler now. 'I appreciate the sentiment. It's just…' He paused, considering the situation further. It wasn't every day that he found himself in such an encounter, and there was something energizing about the spontaneity of it all. 'Actually, it's nice to meet someone new, even if it caught me off guard.'

Marc's eyes lit up, a genuine smile forming on his face. 'I'm glad to hear that. Sometimes the best connections happen when we least expect them.'

'What are you escaping from today? Do you work nearby?' Marc inquired, noting that Nicholas had a satchel overflowing with what appeared to be notebooks and papers.

He responded with a casual exhale, 'Right around the corner.'

'What about you?' Nicholas queried. 'Just down the street. At the library?' Nicholas asked quickly, his words almost snapping back. He then continued, addressing Marc, 'The library?'

Marc nodded, and then his hands instinctively moved to cover his face, a hint of embarrassment clearly evident in his posture. Nicholas noticed the gesture and asked, 'Why the embarrassment?'

With a slight sigh, Marc responded, 'It's just that most people find it quite dreary.' He paused momentarily and continued, 'Most people consider it weird.'

Nicholas offered a reassuring smile and a subtle tilt of his head, conveying his understanding. As Marc's hands slowly lowered from his face, he was met with Nicholas' compassionate gaze, which replaced his embarrassment with a sense of gratitude. Marc's lips curved into a thankful smile, and he expressed, 'Okay no cynicism, no catty remarks.' His feeling of embarrassment began to fade away as he spoke. 'Okay, I work as a research assistant in the young adult section.'

Nicholas' compassion was evident as he steered the conversation. 'You must gain great insights into the literary scene?' Marc's appreciation for Nicholas' understanding and genuine interest in his work increased. 'Absolutely,' he replied with enthusiasm.

As their conversation continued, they delved deeper into the world of words, discussing their favorite authors, the impact of storytelling, and even sharing personal anecdotes about how certain books had influenced their own journeys. With each exchange, a sense of like-mindedness grew, bridging the gap between their initial encounter and the shared interests that now connected them.

Nicholas leaned back in his seat, a contented smile on his lips. 'It's been a while since I've talked about books. You've truly ignited my pleasure for reading.'

Marc's smile mirrored Nicholas'. 'I'm glad to hear that. But I have hogged the conversation—what about you? I, too, see you must do some form of research.'

Nicholas, with a half-smile says, 'I am a human rights attorney'.

Marc, with a tilted head, says, 'Please tell me more.' Nicholas explains that he works for the rights of Hispanic immigrants. As he talks about his career, you can see the passion in his eyes, the enthusiastic tone, and the way his hands unconsciously gesture to emphasize the importance of his work.

'I'm glad you seem interested,' Nicholas replied with genuine appreciation. 'While I may not be immersed in literature like you, I enjoy helping others.'

Marc's eyes widened with intrigue, his head tilting slightly as he leaned in, eager to hear more. 'Human rights attorney? That sounds incredibly impactful.'

Nicholas' half-smile grew full as he recognized Marc's curiosity. 'Of course,' he began, his voice steady and passionate. 'I advocate for the rights of those who can't.'

Marc's gaze remained fixed on Nicholas, a mixture of admiration and something deeper stirring within him. As Nicholas continued to share the details of his work, Marc's thoughts began to shift, a current of desire weaving its way through his consciousness.

He found himself drawn not only to Nicholas' words and the passion that radiated from him but also to the subtle nuances of his expressions—the way his lips moved, the intensity in his eyes, the graceful gestures of his hands.

As Marc observed Nicholas, he noticed his strong and lean build, his warm hazel eyes that seemed to hold endless depth, and the way his dark hair framed his face with a casual yet enticing charm. His well-manicured beard. His smile, with its gentle curve, was like a welcoming invitation, and his overall presence exuded a sense of quiet confidence that drew Marc in. His initial admiration had taken on a more intimate hue, his thoughts dipping into uncharted territory.

As Nicholas' voice resonated in the air, Marc's mind wavered between the conversation and his own internal contemplations. The pull he felt was magnetic, a mixture of intellectual engagement and a burgeoning attraction that he couldn't deny. It was as if the air around them had become charged with a palpable energy that was difficult to ignore.

Despite his professional demeanor and genuine interest in Nicholas' work, Marc found himself wondering what it would be like to be closer, to experience the connection on a different level. His heart raced as he grappled with a sense of exhilaration tinged with apprehension. This newfound desire was unexpected, but it was undeniably real.

Marc's thoughts danced in the realm of what-ifs and maybes, his inner dialog a whirlwind of conflicting emotions. He pondered whether he should reveal his attraction, uncertain of how Nicholas would respond. The idea of crossing that boundary both excited and unnerved him, and he found himself teetering on the edge of a decision.

Marc's gaze held a subtle intensity as the conversation continued to flow between them, an unspoken connection that he wasn't entirely sure Nicholas could sense. He navigated the dichotomy between his professional interest in the conversation and the personal intrigue that tugged at his thoughts. At that moment, the café seemed to hold an electric charge, encapsulating the unspoken tension between them.

As the conversation continued, a subtle shift occurred within Nicholas. While his focus had been firmly rooted in the exchange of ideas, a growing awareness of Marc's presence began to stir something deeper within him. It started as a flicker of something unfamiliar, a subtle recognition of Marc's attractiveness that had previously gone unnoticed.

Nicholas' thoughts began to weave between the conversation and the uncharted territory of his own desires. He found himself more attuned to the nuances of Marc's expressions—the way his lips curved when he smiled, the intensity in his gaze, and the way his laughter seemed to light up the room. The intellectual connection they were forming seemed to blur the lines between strangers and what appeared to be unchartered sexual desires.

A surge of heat rushed through Nicholas as he realized that his thoughts were straying beyond the realm of his fidelity. The realization of his own sexuality seemed to cast a new light on his interactions, revealing a side of himself he hadn't fully explored before. The conversation, once solely about ideas and perspectives, had become a dance of unspoken tension and possibility.

Nicholas felt a mixture of exhilaration and trepidation. He was grappling with a desire that was unfamiliar yet undeniably present. The awareness of his own attraction to Marc was like a door that had been cracked open, revealing a vista of unexplored feelings.

As they continued to talk, Nicholas' attention alternated between Marc's words and the growing awareness of his own yearning. He found himself wondering about the possibilities beyond this conversation, about what it might be like to bridge the gap between intellectual connection and something more intimate. The tension between his genuine admiration for Marc's character and the newfound sexual desire created a swirling vortex of emotions, leaving him both intrigued and uncertain about how to navigate these uncharted waters.

As Nicholas continued to share his insights, his hands unconsciously emphasizing his words, Marc's attention shifted briefly to the glint of a ring on Nicholas' finger—a wedding ring. It was a detail that hadn't registered before, and Marc's thoughts momentarily faltered as he realized the potential implications.

Marc's expression remained neutral, but his internal monolog quickened. The realization of Nicholas' marital status injected a dose of reality into the undercurrents of attraction that had been building between them. His own emotions became a mixture of surprise, disappointment, and an unfamiliar twinge of jealousy.

Still engrossed in the conversation, Nicholas noticed the slight shift in Marc's expression and paused, catching the subtle change. He followed Marc's gaze to his own hand and the ring that rested there. A shadow of realization crossed his features, understanding that his personal life had become part of the equation, even if unintentionally.

Clearing his throat, Nicholas' voice held a hint of sheepishness as he continued, 'Sorry, yes, I'm married.'

For some reason, he felt a need to explain, through a mixture of nervousness and vulnerability in revealing this part of his life to Marc, unsure of how it would be received. And trying to understand why. Why was he embarrassed about this fact?

As Nicholas explained, Marc's expression remained attentive, his gaze steady as he absorbed the unexpected revelation. It was a curveball he hadn't anticipated, and he needed a moment to process the information.

Nicholas' fingers toyed with his coffee cup, a nervous habit that he couldn't shake. He offered a small, apologetic smile, feeling a touch of regret for not addressing this sooner. The weight of his wedding band seemed to grow heavier in that moment, a physical reminder of the commitment he had made. But, again, unsure as to why.

Marc's reaction was a blend of surprise and a wry smile tinged with relief. 'Oh, ok, thanks,' he responded, his tone understanding. 'But that doesn't change the fact that I have enjoyed meeting you. I am sure he or she is lucky…' Marc's voice trailed off, his own thoughts hinting at the potential for something more beyond their coffee shop conversations.

Even before Marc could complete his sentences, Nicholas interpreted, 'She!' He chuckled softly, a mixture of amusement and appreciation in his eyes. It was a lighthearted moment, a glimpse into the friendship that was growing between them despite the unexpected revelation. The realization that Marc's response carried a note of personal investment warmed Nicholas' heart, and he found himself feeling both grateful and intrigued by the way their connection was evolving.

Nicholas' own smile carried a mixture of gratitude and a touch of embarrassment. 'I'm glad to hear that,' he said, his voice carrying a note of sincerity. 'I thought maybe you would have told me to fuck off or something.'

'Nicholas, we're just having a conversation. But who knows what could happen?' Marc shared his thoughts confidentially. Immediately, evaluating his words.

Nicholas' gaze met Marc's, and he could sense the genuine sincerity in his words. The admixture of gratitude and curiosity swirled within him, creating a sense of vulnerability he hadn't anticipated. Marc's openness was refreshing, and it drew him further into the intricate web of their unfolding connection.

Nicholas nodded, his smile softening as he replied, 'I feel a connection, Marc. It's been long since I've just talked with someone.'

Marc's smile mirrored Nicholas', a mix of relief and genuine pleasure. 'I'm glad to hear that,' he responded. 'And I appreciate your honesty about your marital status. It shows a level of respect that's becoming rarer these days.'

Nicholas inclined his head, acknowledging Marc's words. 'Thank you, Marc. It's important to me to be upfront.'

Then, the unexpected request tumbled from Marc's lips, 'I don't want to cause problems, but could I see you again?' Can we do that? Coffee?' And Nicholas found himself momentarily taken aback. The suggestion of meeting again for coffee was both enticing and laden with complexities. Nicholas' mind raced as he considered the implications, his desire to continue the connection warring with the potential complications.

His voice blended contemplation and honesty as he replied, 'I appreciate your straightforwardness, Marc. I won't deny that I've enjoyed our conversation, but I want to respect both situations. Meeting again sounds appealing, but I need time to think about it.'

Marc's response was understanding, his gaze steady as he met Nicholas' eyes. 'Of course, take your time. I wouldn't want to rush into anything.'

Nicholas' gratitude for Marc's understanding was all over his face. 'Thanks for being cool about this. Let me mull it over, and maybe we will meet here again.' Marc replied, 'I am usually here every afternoon.'

Amid the café's lively atmosphere, they had an unmistakable connection. It was a moment filled with the potential for more than friendship, a delightful blend of attraction, mutual respect, and the unpredictable twists of life. In that very moment, they were two individuals embarking on the intricate journey of human connection, united by their shared pursuit of an unlikely friendship.

In the midst of the café's vibrant atmosphere, Nicholas and Marc's unspoken bond persisted, echoing the potential for a deeper connection. Their shared desires for authenticity and understanding wove a delicate thread between them, as they navigated the complexities of their feelings amidst the hum of life around them.

Chapter 2

Café Sorrows

Nicholas sat at his usual corner table in the coffee shop, his fingers tracing absent-minded patterns on the ceramic surface of his cup. The familiar aroma of freshly brewed coffee enveloped him, mingling with the subdued hum of conversation and the occasional clatter of dishes. It was a place of refuge—a sanctuary where he could escape the noise of his own thoughts, if only for a little while.

As the soft chime of the café's bell announced the new arrivals, Nicholas' gaze remained distant, his mind wrapped in introspection. His first encounter with Marc had been a spark that had ignited something within him, a realization that his life had been missing something, something that felt increasingly vital as the days went by.

The anticipation of a second chance meeting with Marc had driven Nicholas back to the café. He had hoped for another opportunity to connect, to delve into the uncharted territory of shared conversations and burgeoning emotions. But as the minutes ticked by, each tick echoing in the chambers of his thoughts, he realized that Marc wasn't entering the door. Disappointment tugged at his chest, and he exhaled a sigh he hadn't even realized he was holding.

His mind drifted back to the day he had stood before his wife, Brooke, exchanging vows. He remembered the sunlight filtering through stained glass windows, casting a warm glow over her radiant smile. In that moment, love and hope had danced in his heart. He had meant every word he had spoken, every promise he had made. Brooke was a wonderful woman, kind, and understanding.

The day they took vows in front of family and friends was etched in his consciousness like an old photograph, its colors vivid and its emotions tangible. He remembered the sunlight filtering through stained glass windows, casting a warm, ethereal glow over her radiant smile. At that moment, love and hope had danced in his heart, a symphony of emotions that had resonated through every fiber of his being.

The vows they had exchanged had been more than words; they were promises woven with dreams and aspirations. He had gazed into Brooke's eyes, seeing a future that stretched out before them—a future filled with laughter, shared adventures, and a love that would withstand the tests of time. He had meant every word he had spoken, every promise he had made. Brooke was a wonderful woman, fiercely supporting him in every way. The memory of her unwavering presence in his life filled him with a profound sense of gratitude.

Their wedding day had been a celebration of their love, a culmination of months of planning and anticipation. He recalled the joyous laughter that had echoed through the air, the touch of her hand in his as they danced for the first time as husband and wife. It was a day brimming with happiness, the love of family and friends surrounding them like a warm embrace. Their smiles had been genuine, their hearts alight with the promise of a shared future.

But even amid the celebration, a subtle shadow had crept into his heart. It was a shadow he had brushed aside, a whisper of doubt that he had chosen to ignore. The day had been magical, yet a part of him wondered if the magic was only skin-deep, if the happiness they projected was a veneer that masked the complexities beneath.

Then, their most intimate public moment, their first kiss as husband and wife—a moment that should have been filled with the magic of a newfound union, a kiss that should have ignited a flame of passion. Yet, as their lips met, he felt an unexpected sadness, a hollowness that he couldn't comprehend. It wasn't that he didn't love Brooke; he did, profoundly. But the spark he had hoped for, the intensity that had been absent in that moment, had left him feeling strangely detached.

His thoughts meandered through these memories, threading together the tapestry of his relationship with Brooke. She deserved more than he was capable of giving, and he couldn't escape the realization that his heart was yearning for something he had yet to fully understand. The encounter with Marc had stirred emotions he hadn't known were dormant within him, emotions that beckoned him toward uncharted territory.

Nicholas' fingers played idly with the edge of his wedding band, the cold metal a reminder of the commitment he had made. He pondered the complexities of his feelings, the journey of self-discovery that had led him to this moment. Brooke deserved honesty, and he couldn't continue to suppress the truth he was uncovering within himself. It wasn't just about him; it was about honoring the love they shared, even if it meant confronting painful decisions.

As he gazed out of the café window, the world beyond blurred, and his thoughts swirled in a vortex of uncertainty. He yearned for clarity, for a path forward that would respect both his own desires and Brooke's well-being. The sun cast long shadows on the pavement, a metaphor for the intricacies of his heart and the choices he would have to make.

With a sigh, Nicholas pushed back from the table, his heart heavy with the weight of his internal struggles. The café, once a place of refuge, now felt like a mirror reflecting the complexity of his emotions. But as time passed, the path he had chosen felt more like a detour—one that took him away from his own desires and longings. The wedding band that encircled his finger was more than a piece of jewelry; it was a constant reminder of the commitment he had made. Yet lately, it had begun to feel like a shackle, binding him to a life that no longer resonated with the truth he was uncovering within himself.

Nicholas sighed, his gaze distant as he stared into the depths of his coffee. The steam curled and dissipated, much like his own emotions. Was he beginning to be dishonest, not just with himself, but with Brooke as well? The thought weighed heavily on him, a growing cloud of uncertainty overshadowing his once-clear path.

His fingers brushed against the cool metal of his wedding band, and he closed his eyes momentarily, a sigh escaping his lips as he grappled with the turmoil in his heart. The journey of self-discovery he had embarked on was a labyrinthine one, its passages winding through the depths of his soul, unravelling the threads of his desires and fears. He had been living in a haze, an existence painted by societal expectations, while denying the truth that had been steadily gaining strength within him.

Opening his eyes, he found himself observing two men walking by, their hands entwined with a natural ease that bespoke a profound connection. Their intimacy, an expression of love uninhibited by judgment, struck a chord within him. Nicholas felt a pang of envy, not for their relationship specifically, but for the authenticity they portrayed—the freedom to embrace love as it was meant to be.

As the couple's laughter floated in the air, Nicholas' thoughts wandered back to his own past. Memories of his proposal to Brooke flooded his mind—roses, candles, and the nervous flutter in his chest as he had asked her to share her life with him. He had meant every word, yet in the face of his evolving self-awareness, he questioned whether he had been true to both her and himself.

The echoes of their wedding day resounded in his memory—the radiant smiles, the vows spoken with earnestness, and the collective joy of their loved ones. It had been a day of celebration, of dreams realized, and love acknowledged. And yet, beneath the surface, Nicholas had sensed the faint tremors of his own internal conflict, like a crack in the facade of perfection.

The memory of their first kiss as a married couple held an unexpected sadness. It had been a culmination of their promises, the moment their futures had merged. Yet, even in the tender press of lips against lips, he had felt a dissonance—a discord between the outward expression and the inner truth. The sadness he had felt then was an early whisper of the turmoil he now faced.

The couple's presence triggered a longing within Nicholas—a yearning to cast off the layers of denial, to walk hand in hand with someone without pretense. Their unabashed affection was a stark realization of the life he wished to live, a life free from the confines of expectations he had willingly embraced. As he looked up and gave them a slightly twisted smile.

Nicholas took a deep breath, the air filling his lungs with a sense of resolve as he stepped out into the bustling street, he felt a mixture of determination and trepidation. The journey ahead would be anything but easy, but he knew that facing his own truth was the only way to navigate the labyrinth of his heart. With the couple now fading from view, he turned his gaze toward the café where his journey had begun. In that place, he had found a connection that had opened his eyes to his own desires, a connection that had awakened him from his self-imposed slumber.

Determined to navigate the labyrinth of his heart, he knew that the path ahead was uncertain that it would challenge him in ways he couldn't predict. But he also knew that he couldn't deny his truth any longer. As he walked away from the scene, the weight of his wedding band seemed to lighten, as if in acknowledgment of his burgeoning authenticity. The journey of self-discovery was far from over, but he was finally taking steps toward embracing the truth that had been waiting to blossom within him.

With each passing minute, the burden of his thoughts grew increasingly suffocating. He stole a final look at the entrance of the café, a glimmer of hope tethering him to the possibility of Marc's presence. Yet, as the minutes ticked by, that hope dimmed, giving way to a somber acknowledgment of the reality.

As he continued to stroll down the street, his gaze landed on a library, a wave of warmth washing over him. Nestled beside it, an open florist.

Nicholas found himself standing before the florist's window display, the vibrant blooms arrayed in a kaleidoscope of colors and shapes. He knew he needed to make a choice, but he was paralyzed by indecision. In the past, ordering flowers had been a straightforward task—red roses for romantic occasions, lilies for sympathy, and tulips for cheerful greetings. But this, this was uncharted territory

He rubbed his temples, attempting to clear the mental fog that had settled over him. A flurry of questions swirled in his mind.

What kind of flowers would be suitable for this situation? What message did he want to convey to Marc? And perhaps most perplexing of all, what did Marc even like?

Nicholas had never delved into the realm of same-sex relationships before, nor had he explored the intricacies of being interested in a man. He had no reference point, no clichéd movie scene to emulate. The thought of picking out flowers for a guy filled him with both uncertainty and intrigue.

He entered the florist, the delicate aroma of blossoms enveloping him. An elderly woman with silver hair stood behind the counter, her eyes crinkling with kindness as she smiled at Nicholas.

'Hello there, dear. How can I help you?' she asked, her voice a soothing melody.

Nicholas hesitated, his gaze drifting to the sea of flowers surrounding him. 'I, uh, I need to buy some flowers,' he stammered.

The florist's warm smile never wavered. 'Of course, dear. Flowers can speak volumes when words fail. Is this for a special occasion?'

Nicholas glanced down at his trembling hands, then back at the florist. 'It's, um, it's complicated. I'm not sure what would be appropriate.'

Understanding washed over the florist's features, and she beckoned Nicholas closer. 'Well, dear, let's start by thinking about what this person means to you. Are you trying to convey love, friendship, or perhaps an apology?'

Nicholas sighed, grateful for her guidance. 'It's a bit of everything, really: love, friendship, and hope.'

The florist nodded knowingly. 'Ah, a bouquet with layers of sentiment. How beautiful! Let's choose some flowers to show how you feel.'

She led Nicholas through the aisles, explaining the

significance of each bloom. Roses, she said, were the universal language of love, but they came in various colors, each carrying its own message. He decided on a mix of red and white roses—red for love and white for friendship. To convey his hope, the florist suggested he add some delicate lilies, symbolizing renewal and hope.

Nicholas watched as the florist expertly arranged the flowers into a bouquet. He couldn't help but marvel at how effortlessly she navigated the world of emotions through petals and stems. It was a skill he had never appreciated before.

As she tied a ribbon around the bouquet, Nicholas' mind wandered back to Marc. He thought of their stolen moments in the café, their whispered confessions of love, and the passion they had shared in secret. His heart ached with longing and regret, but he was determined to make amends.

Nicholas asked, 'Can I have them delivered next door to the library, tomorrow?'

The sweet lady said, 'Yes, of course. And who will they be going to?'

Nicholas stopped for a moment, confused, 'Oh, yes, Marc Anders.'

'And how will you be paying? And can you please complete the invoice form with your name and address, and the card?'

Nicholas pulled out a credit card from his wallet and handed to the lady in exchange for a pen. He completed the paperwork and handed it back to the lovely lady.

Nicholas thanked the florist and she replied with pleasantries. Nicholas, with a smile on his face, turned and left the shop. The sun hung low in the sky, casting a warm, golden hue over the city streets as he pondered what tomorrow would bring.

Chapter 3

Beans, Laughter, and Heart-to-Hearts

The library, which was Marc's sanctuary, was a realm of knowledge and solitude that provided respite from the chaos of the outside world. Amid the hushed whispers of pages turning and the gentle scent of old books, he found a space for his thoughts to roam freely.

As he settled into a worn leather chair, his mind replayed the encounter with Nicholas at the coffee shop—the way their eyes had met, the electric spark of connection, the depth of their conversation. It was a moment that had left an indelible mark on his heart, a chapter he couldn't help but revisit time and again.

His yearning to return to that coffee shop gnawed at him—a fleeting desire to catch another glimpse of Nicholas' warm smile. Yet, as he sat there, his fingers tracing the edges of a book cover, a heavy truth weighed him down. Nicholas was married, a fact that bore a weight of its own, one that Marc couldn't ignore no matter how strongly his heart pulled him.

Every afternoon, he would stand at the crossroads, the café's entrance mere steps away, his heart warring with his conscience. He'd picture Nicholas there, sipping his coffee, his eyes lifting to meet Marc's. The desire to rekindle their connection tugged at him like a persistent whisper, urging him to act on his feelings.

But each day, Marc would take a step back, shaking his head to dispel the temptation. The voice of reason echoed in his mind, reminding him that Nicholas was a married man—a life entangled with another, a commitment Marc couldn't and wouldn't intrude upon.

The weeks passed, and with each ticking second, Marc's desperation deepened. The longing he harbored for Nicholas was more than a mere pang; it was a relentless ache that clung to him, infiltrating every aspect of his daily life. The library's quiet corners, once a haven of comfort, had transformed into chambers of whispered torment, echoing his unspoken desires and unfulfilled wishes.

As he shelved books and assisted library visitors, Marc found his thoughts consistently drifting toward Nicholas. It was as if the man's presence had left an indelible mark on his consciousness, impossible to erase. The connection they had forged during their initial encounter had left a chasm within him, a void that yearned to be filled with more moments, more conversations, more stolen glances that held worlds of meaning.

He questioned himself incessantly—his desires, his yearnings, and the decision he had made to restrain himself. It was a chaotic whirlwind of emotions, a storm within his chest that seemed to intensify with each passing day. Doubts and insecurities gnawed at him, like shadows lurking at the edges of his consciousness.

Marc's internal monolog was a symphony of conflicting emotions. He yearned to see Nicholas again, to bask in the warmth of his presence, to delve into those captivating conversations that had sparked a fire within his heart. But the knowledge of Nicholas' marriage was a weight that dragged him down, a reminder of boundaries he had no right to cross.

The memory of that fateful day at the coffee shop was etched in his mind like a vivid painting—a tapestry of emotions, glances exchanged, and the connection that had been palpable even in the midst of strangers. The café had been a place of serendipity, a crossroads that had brought their paths together, however fleetingly. And yet, in the face of his longing, Marc found himself trapped in a bittersweet limbo.

He pondered the possibility of returning to the café, of trying to capture another chance moment. But reason battled against his desires. It wasn't just about him; it was about respecting the commitments others had made. As much as he yearned for Nicholas, he didn't want to be a catalyst for chaos, pain, or the upheaval of a marriage.

The library, a haven of knowledge and introspection, offered him refuge from the chaos of his emotions. But even within its hallowed walls, Marc couldn't escape the memories that had intertwined with his longing for Nicholas. Each shelf, each book seemed to bear the weight of his unspoken emotions, as if they had taken on a life of their own.

Then, on a day like any other, Marc's world was gently shaken. A bouquet of flowers arrived at the library, accompanied by a note that held both hope and trepidation. 'To Marc, let's have a coffee,' the note read, with a small heart drawn at the bottom, a visual representation of the connection that had sparked between them.

The simple gesture sent ripples through his being, stirring a whirlwind of emotions within him. The sight of those flowers was like a beacon of light, a glimmer of possibility that illuminated the darkness of his doubts. A surge of warmth enveloped him, a mixture of excitement and uncertainty that pulsed through his veins.

Marc clutched the note, his heart pounding as he considered the implications. It was an invitation, a whisper of opportunity, a chance to see Nicholas once more. But with that opportunity came a tumultuous sea of emotions—hope, fear, guilt, desire—each wave crashing against the shore of his consciousness.

As he stared at the flowers and the note, Marc's mind was a whirlwind of thoughts. Could he allow himself this chance? Could he justify meeting Nicholas, knowing the complications that lay between them? He wrestled with his conscience, with the longing that had consumed him, and with the very real possibility of irrevocably altering the course of his own life.

With the note still in his hand, Marc gazed out of the library window, his thoughts consumed by the choices that lay ahead. The flowers on his desk symbolized more than a simple invitation; they represented a crossroads, a moment of decision that would shape his path. The mournfulness that had colored his days was now mingled with the glimmer of hope, a hope that carried the potential to either heal or break his heart.

As the library's quiet ambiance enveloped him, Marc knew that the choice was his to make. The invitation lay before him, a catalyst for change, a potential turning point that would shape the course of their lives. With a deep breath, he pocketed the note, the weight of the flowers a reminder of the feelings he had nurtured in the shadows.

As he left the library, Marc's steps were purposeful, his heart a mix of uncertainty and hope. The coffee shop, once a place of longing, had transformed into a threshold of possibility. The path ahead was unclear, but for the first time in weeks, Marc felt a glimmer of courage—the courage to confront his own desires, to embrace the unexpected, and to navigate the uncharted territory of his heart.

He texts his friend Sam:

Marc: *Where are you?*

Sam: *I am at the Coffee Rainbow.*

Marc: *I'll be there in ten.*

Marc nearly runs to the coffee shop, and at his pace, he probably shaved off a good two minutes from his usual route. As he turned the corner, the familiar and welcoming aroma of freshly roasted coffee beans enveloped him, lifting his spirits. The enticing scent seemed to guide him like a compass, leading him toward the café not unlike where destiny had intertwined his path with Nicholas'.

He entered the cozy establishment, a sense of déjà vu washing over him as he spotted the corner table—a table like the one where that encounter had occurred with Nicholas. It was as if the universe had conspired to recreate that serendipitous moment, granting him a chance to reclaim that sense of connection he had found with Nicholas. Marc took a deep breath, his heart beating in anticipation, as he stepped further into the café, ready to see where this unexpected journey would take him.

Marc sat across from his best friend Sam at their favorite café, a comforting aroma of freshly brewed coffee filling the air. Sam, with his warm smile and expressive eyes, exuded an air of approachability that made it easy for Marc to open up about anything.

'So spill the beans,' Sam said playfully, taking a sip of his dark roast. 'You've been walking around with a secret smile for weeks now. What's got you all giddy?'

Marc chuckled, a mixture of excitement and nervousness dancing in his eyes. 'Okay, okay, I'll spill. You remember that coffee shop I told you about?'

Sam's eyes widened with curiosity, and he leaned in, his

interest piqued. 'Yeah, of course! That's where you met your mysterious coffee-shop guy, right? The one you can't stop thinking about?'

Marc nodded, a sheepish grin tugging at his lips. 'Exactly. Well, guess what? He sent me flowers and a note inviting me for coffee again.'

Sam's face lit up with a mischievous grin. 'Oh! Look at you, Mr. Mysterious Coffee Date Guy! Are you going to spill the beans on your secret admirer?'

Marc laughed, shaking his head. 'I wish it were that simple, Sam. He's married. It's complicated.' His laughter held a touch of wistfulness, as if he wished things could be as straightforward as Sam suggested. The complexities of his feelings for Nicholas seemed to echo in his words, a reminder of the tangled emotions that had taken root within him.

Sam's expression softened with understanding. 'Ah, the plot thickens. Complicated, huh? Well, you know, life can never be easy.'

Marc sighed, sipping his coffee as he contemplated Sam's words. 'Yeah, I know. It's just... I can't shake this feeling. We had such a connection, you know? And it's like I'm stuck in this limbo, wanting to see him again but feeling guilty at the same time.'

Sam reached out and placed a reassuring hand on Marc's. 'Marc, you're allowed to feel conflicted. Love and attraction, they're not always neat and tidy. But remember, your feelings matter too. Just take it slow and easy, and whatever happens, know that I've got your back.'

Marc sighed, his gaze fixated on the swirling patterns in his coffee. 'Thanks. It's just... I can't help but feel guilty about this whole situation. I mean, Nicholas is married, and I don't want to be the cause of any pain or turmoil.'

Sam nodded, understanding in his eyes. 'I get it, Marc.

Falling for a married man—it's a complicated and tricky path to navigate. There's no denying that.'

A mix of frustration and sadness crossed Marc's features. 'Exactly. I don't want to be the reason someone's marriage falls apart, you know? And what if he's just having a moment of weakness? I don't want to be a rebound or something like that.'

Sam leaned back in his chair, his expression thoughtful. 'You're right to think about those things. It's crucial to be aware of the potential pitfalls. Falling for someone who's already committed can lead to a world of hurt—for all parties involved.'

Marc's voice carried a tinge of bitterness. 'I know. It's like I'm stuck between wanting to explore this connection and being held back by this moral dilemma.'

Sam's gaze softened, his voice gentle. 'Marc, it's important to acknowledge your feelings, but also to recognize the reality of the situation. You're not wrong for having emotions, but you need to be honest with yourself about the potential consequences.'

'I know,' Marc replied, his shoulders slumping. 'But it's so damn complicated. I wish there were clear answers.'

Sam offered a sympathetic smile. 'Life rarely hands us clear answers, my friend. But what you can do is prioritize your own well-being. Don't neglect your own feelings in this equation. If you're going to navigate this path, do it with your eyes wide open.'

A sigh escaped Marc's lips. 'It's just hard to ignore the heart, you know? Especially when you've felt such a strong connection. I am obsessed, he is in my thoughts all the time.' As Marc lowers his head into his hands and shakes it left to right.

Sam's expression turned more serious. 'I get it, Marc. But remember, sometimes the strongest connections are also the ones that can lead us astray. Just make sure you're not sacrificing your own happiness for the sake of someone else's. You deserve that great love too.'

The weight of Sam's words settled over Marc like a heavy blanket. He knew Sam was right, but it didn't make the situation any less agonizing. 'Thanks for being the voice of reason. I needed that.'

Sam squeezed Marc's hand reassuringly. 'That's what friends are for, right? Just promise me one thing: whatever you decide, make sure it's a decision that respects your own heart.'

Marc nodded, a mixture of gratitude and uncertainty swirling within him. As he gazed at Sam, he was reminded of the value of having someone who could provide clarity in the midst of emotional turmoil. The conversation was a reminder that while the path ahead was uncertain, he wasn't alone in navigating it.

Marc's gaze softened as he met Sam's eyes. 'Thanks, Sam. You always know how to put things into perspective. And speaking of perspective, how's your latest case at the shelter?'

Sam's face lit up with passion as he launched into a discussion about his work as a social worker at a local shelter.

The conversation flowed seamlessly between them, laughter and camaraderie weaving through their words. They shared stories of triumphs and challenges, leaning on each other for support and guidance.

As their conversation continued, Marc felt a deep sense of gratitude for having Sam in his life. Sam's understanding and empathy were a balm to his soul, helping him navigate the complexities of his feelings for Nicholas. They teased each other, joked about their own romantic escapades, and dished out friendly advice.

'You know,' Sam said with a twinkle in his eye, 'you're

lucky to have such a romantic coffee shop story. I mean, mine are usually just me tripping over my own feet or spilling coffee all over myself.'

Marc laughed, shaking his head. 'Oh, please, Sam. You're a total catch. I've seen the way people look at you.'

Sam shrugged, a hint of bashfulness coloring his cheeks. 'Well, maybe I'll find my coffee shop mystery person someday. But for now, I'm living vicariously through your story. Just promise me you'll follow your heart, okay?'

Marc smiled warmly at Sam, feeling a renewed sense of determination. 'I promise. And I'll make sure to keep you updated on all the coffee shop drama.'

Their laughter filled the café, a testament to the deep bond they shared. As the evening sunlight filtered through the windows, Marc felt a renewed sense of hope. With Sam by his side, he knew he could navigate the complexities of his feelings for Nicholas, one cup of coffee at a time. As he pulled the note from his pocket to look at it one more time, rereading the note, there was one word that he had neglected and overlooked: 'tomorrow?'

Chapter 4

Unraveling Secrets

The aroma of freshly brewed coffee filled the air as Nicholas sat at the corner table, his heart racing with anticipation and uncertainty. He had hoped that his gesture would spark that chance—second meeting with Marc—a chance encounter that wasn't entirely left to 'chance'. He recalled the stirring connection he had felt from their first meeting, and the desire to explore it further had led him to this moment.

The days had turned into weeks since that initial encounter. The memory of their conversation had lingered in Nicholas' thoughts, fueling his curiosity and prompting him to visit the café whenever he could steal a moment away.

During the weeks that had passed, Nicholas had navigated a tumultuous emotional landscape. His heart wrestled with conflicting feelings, and his mind raced with questions about his marriage, his desires, and the path he was considering. He found himself caught in a tangle of past decisions and present possibilities, each choice carrying its own weight of consequences.

Nicholas' conversations with Brooke, his wife, had become strained as he grappled with his internal turmoil. Their interactions were laced with tension, and he felt the weight of guilt for keeping his inner struggles hidden. The marriage that had once seemed solid now felt fragile, its foundation shaken by the awakening of desires he had long suppressed.

Yet, despite the emotional upheaval, Nicholas' heart remained tethered to the memory of Marc—the way he had listened intently, the sparks of shared understanding, and the vulnerability that had bloomed during their conversation. He had become entranced by the possibility of something new, something that held the promise of authenticity and connection.

And so, on this day, Nicholas found himself back in the café, his heart racing with both hope and trepidation. He had taken a step toward self-discovery, but the path ahead was uncharted and filled with uncertainties. Would Marc appear? Would their connection deepen or fade?

As Nicholas sat at that corner table, his gaze scanning the entrance with a mixture of anticipation and nerves, he reflected on the changes that had begun to unfurl within him. The past few weeks had been a journey of introspection, a journey that had challenged him to confront his true desires and the complexities of his identity.

He took a deep breath, his fingers tapping rhythmically on the tabletop. Whether Marc walked through that door or not, the mere fact that he was here, willing to embrace the unknown, was a testament to his growing courage and the yearning to explore the depths of his heart.

Nicholas' thoughts swirled, a whirlwind of emotions, memories, and possibilities. He had taken the first steps toward unraveling the secrets within himself, and in doing so, he had set in motion a series of events that would forever alter the course of his life.

When Nicholas sat across from Marc, his gaze fixed on the intricate play of emotions dancing across his face, he couldn't help but reflect on the depth of his attraction. He had been drawn to Marc from the moment they had met by 'chance.' The initial conversation had ignited a spark within him—a spark that had grown into a full-blown fire, consuming his thoughts and awakening desires he had long suppressed. But what was it about Marc that had triggered such a powerful reaction within him?

Nicholas' mind unraveled the layers, tracing back to the allure that had first caught his attention. It was more than just Marc's physical appearance, though that was undeniably a part of it. There was an authenticity about Marc, a genuine openness and warmth that had made Nicholas feel seen and heard in a way he hadn't experienced in a long time.

The more they had talked, the more Nicholas had sensed a shared journey of self-discovery and authenticity. Marc's willingness to share his own experiences, his vulnerability in revealing his identity as a gay individual, had created a bridge of understanding between them. It was a bridge that had allowed Nicholas to explore his own desires, and confront the truths he had hidden away.

Marc's confidence and assuredness had intrigued Nicholas, but it was also his compassion and empathy that had struck a chord. The way Marc had listened intently to his revelations about his marriage and his life made Nicholas feel accepted and understood. It was a feeling that had been missing from his life for far too long.

The intimate moment they had shared had solidified the attraction Nicholas had been grappling with. It was a raw, unfiltered glimpse into the chemistry that existed between them, a chemistry that he couldn't ignore.

Nicholas' thoughts swirled in a whirlwind of contemplation as he thought of Marc. He realized that his attraction went beyond the physical—it was a combination of Marc's personality, his shared experiences, and the unspoken connection they had formed. The authenticity and vulnerability they both displayed had forged a unique bond, one that had the power to grow into something new, fresh.

As the café's ambient sounds faded into the background, Nicholas' thoughts remained fixed on Marc. There was a sense of wonder in his eyes, a curiosity about the future he was now embarking upon. It was a journey of self-discovery, of rewriting his narrative, and of embracing the desires that had long been suppressed.

In Marc, Nicholas had found a mirror to his own desires, a guide to navigating the complexities of his identity. With every beat of his heart, he understood that this connection was both a challenge and a gift—a chance to finally be honest with himself and to pursue the path of authenticity, no matter where it led.

As Nicholas stared out the window, he heard the soft chime of the door. As Marc entered the café, Nicholas' heart skipped a beat. He had been seated at the corner table, his anticipation building with each passing moment. His eyes had been trained on the café's entrance, a mixture of hope and uncertainty swirling within him.

When Marc's familiar figure finally came into view, Nicholas' breath caught in his throat. There was a sense of magnetism that pulled his gaze toward Marc, a force he couldn't fully explain. His heart raced as their eyes met and a warmth spread through his chest.

A genuine smile curved Nicholas' lips as Marc's gaze settled on him. In that instant, a wave of relief washed over him. The mere presence of Marc, spark that something inside of him, those feelings that were so unfamiliar, but feelings that felt safe.

The past few weeks had been a whirlwind of emotions for Nicholas—a journey of self-discovery and contemplation about his desires and the path he wanted to take. And now, as Marc approached the table, Nicholas' heart swelled with a mixture of gratitude and anticipation.

In Marc's warm smile and the excitement that danced in his gaze, Nicholas found a sense of relief. It was as if Marc's presence validated the choices he had been wrestling with, affirming that he was not alone in his quest for authenticity.

Before Marc entered the café, his eyes instinctively scanned the room, searching for the familiar face that had occupied his thoughts over the past few weeks. There was a mix of excitement and uncertainty bubbling within him, a sense of curiosity about the connection they had formed.

And then, his gaze settled on Nicholas—seated, his presence both reassuring and magnetic. Marc's heart did a little leap, and a gentle smile played on his lips as he absorbed the scene in front of him.

In that moment, his first thoughts were a swirl of recognition and anticipation. He recognized the significance of this encounter, the way their paths had aligned once again. The sense of familiarity that had started with their chance meeting had transformed into something more—a genuine desire to know Nicholas better, to unravel the layers of his thoughts and emotions.

The warmth of Nicholas' smile as their eyes met sent a shiver of excitement down Marc's spine. It was a smile that held a promise of shared moments, conversations that transcended the ordinary, and the potential for something meaningful to blossom between them.

Approaching the table, Marc's mind buzzed with a mix of excitement and curiosity. What kind of stories would unfold today? What bits of each other's lives would they uncover?

Could their bond keep growing, or would real-world complexities pose challenges?

But amid the uncertainties, Marc's heart felt light. Chatting with Nicholas, his heart danced with thanks and optimism—grateful for this chance to see Nicholas again, and hopeful for the potential of what might come next. Each step to the table was like turning a page, diving into a new chapter full of exciting possibilities.

As Marc greeted him with those simple yet meaningful words, 'Nicholas, it's good to see you again,' Nicholas felt a spark of connection. Marc's genuine enthusiasm resonated with him on a profound level, and he couldn't help but respond with a sense of sincerity.

'You too,' Nicholas replied, his own smile infused with a touch of relief. It was a moment of connection that went beyond surface-level interactions. In Marc's presence, Nicholas found a safe space to explore his emotions and desires, a space where he could be himself without pretense or expectation.

Their exchange was a dance of unspoken emotions, a silent understanding that their connection was more than chance—it was the convergence of two souls on a journey of discovery, longing, and possibility. As they settled into their conversation, Nicholas' heart remained open to the unfolding of this unexpected chapter in his life.

Their talk flowed naturally, and as they sipped their coffee, Marc found the courage to broach a topic that had been on his mind. 'By the way, Nicholas, I wanted to thank you for the flowers. They were a sweet surprise.' He glanced at the small vase of flowers on the table, a genuine smile gracing his lips.

Nicholas returned the smile, his eyes radiating warmth. 'You're welcome. I'm really glad you enjoyed them. It was just a small way to brighten your day.'

Marc's lips curved into a teasing grin. 'Mission

accomplished, then.' As he spoke, his expression took on a more contemplative air. 'To be honest, I was surprised and moved by that. I mean, I wanted to respect your situation, but I also really wanted to acknowledge the connection I thought we had.'

Nicholas chuckled softly. 'You know, it's a bit ironic—I've made it a routine to come here almost every day, hoping to catch a glimpse of you walking through those doors.' He offered a wistful smile. 'But most days, I'd leave feeling a little emptier.'

Marc's eyebrows lifted in surprise, a mixture of emotions flickering across his face. 'And here I've been actively avoiding this place, feeling almost guilty about it now.' He let out a small, self-deprecating laugh. 'Guess I'll need to reevaluate my choices.'

Marc leaned back in his chair, a mixture of vulnerability and honesty in his gaze. 'Because coming here meant there was a chance of seeing you.'

Nicholas' expression softened, his eyes locking onto Marc's. 'I know, Marc. I'm aware that I bring a lot of complications into the mix.' He hesitated for a moment, then added, 'But you're not alone in that. I have my own insecurities, my own doubts.'

Marc's gaze held a mixture of curiosity and empathy. 'Such as?'

Nicholas' smile faded slightly, and he looked down at his coffee cup before meeting Marc's eyes again. 'Such as wondering if I'm being dishonest with myself and with Brooke. Such as worrying if pursuing something with you means I'm betraying the life I've built.'

Marc's voice was soft and understanding. 'I get it. Those are big questions, and they deserve serious consideration.'

Nicholas nodded, a blend of earnestness and apprehension in his gaze. 'I just want you to know that I'm not taking this lightly, Marc. I would like to get to know you, but I don't want to hurt anyone in the process.'

Their eyes locked, a bridge of vulnerability connecting them in that moment. Their exchange was a testament to their shared complexities, a reminder that their connection wasn't just about attraction—it was about grappling with life's uncertainties and finding a way forward.

More relaxed now, they settled into their seats, the atmosphere felt charged with possibility. The conversation flowed naturally, a blend of shared interests, personal anecdotes, and laughter. Nicholas found himself drawn into Marc's world, his perspective on life, and the genuine authenticity that radiated from him.

As the afternoon sunlight streamed through the café windows, the conversation took a more introspective turn. Nicholas leaned in slightly, his voice taking on a more subdued tone. 'Marc, there's something I need to share with you. Our meeting has made me realize the importance of honesty.'

Marc's gaze locked onto Nicholas', sensing the gravity of his words. 'I'm listening,' he replied in an encouraging tone.

Nicholas took a deep breath, the weight of his past and present pressing on his chest. 'I've been married to Brooke for over two years.' He paused, allowing the revelation to settle between them. 'I need you to understand this isn't something I take lightly. I've been grappling with suppressed desires, and meeting you has brought those feelings to the surface.'

Marc's expression remained empathetic, his gaze a mixture of understanding and compassion. 'Nicholas, I appreciate your honesty. It takes a lot to open up.'

As Nicholas' words hung in the air, his mind drifted back to the past, a montage of memories and emotions flashing before him. He recalled the pressures he had faced, the societal expectations that had guided his choices. Flashbacks of moments spent with Brooke punctuated his thoughts—a reminder of the commitment he had made but also the internal struggle he had tried to bury.

In his younger years, Nicholas had embarked on a journey of self-discovery, exploring the intricacies of his own desires. It had been a tumultuous path, one marked by confusion and societal expectations. The decision to marry Brooke had been, in part, an attempt to suppress the true nature of his desires, to conform to the world's norms.

Across the table, Marc's thoughts mirrored Nicholas' introspection. He understood the complexity of the situation, having walked his own path of self-acceptance and coming out. Marc's own experiences growing up as a gay individual had shaped his outlook on life. He remembered the anxiety of revealing his true self to family and friends, the weight of expectation, and the relief that came with embracing his identity.

Marc's voice cut through the silence, his tone compassionate. 'Nicholas, I totally get where you're coming from. I mean, facing your own authentic self can be a real rollercoaster, especially with all those hopes that is expected, things are better, but…'

The aroma of freshly brewed coffee mingled with the hum of conversation around them, creating a cozy atmosphere as Nicholas and Marc resettled into their seats. Their easy camaraderie was evident in the way their words flowed, each sentence building upon the connection they had formed.

As their conversation continued, Nicholas found himself sharing more about his life, including his marriage to Brooke. He spoke with a mix of candor and introspection, revealing the intricacies of their relationship and the challenges he had faced in reconciling his true desires.

'Brooke is an amazing woman,' Nicholas concluded, a thoughtful expression on his face. 'Throughout our marriage, she's been supportive in so many ways.'

Marc nodded, his gaze fixed on Nicholas. 'It's clear that you care about her a lot.'

Nicholas' lips curved into a small smile, appreciating Marc's understanding. 'Yes, I do. She's been a significant part of my life.'

Marc's reply was positive, yet a subtle hint of jealousy lingered beneath the surface. 'It's wonderful to have someone who's there for you,' he said, his tone unclear. 'To share your journey with.'

As Marc spoke, his mind wandered to the thought of another person in Nicholas' life—a person who held a deep connection with him, who knew his thoughts and feelings in a way that Marc was only beginning to discover. It was a feeling he hadn't expected, this twinge of possessiveness that flitted through his thoughts.

Nicholas caught the fleeting expression in Marc's eyes, the subtle shift in his demeanor. He sensed a hint of something unspoken, a complexity that mirrored his own feelings. The moment hung between them, heavy with the weight of unsaid words and unexplored emotions.

Even though a twinge of jealousy lingered, Marc's gaze held its ground, his smile as real as it gets. He truly understood Nicholas' trepidation about Brooke, even as he sorted through his own feelings. It was like a reality check on the revolving cycle of the human condition—how emotions could both pump you up and throw you off balance—and how these unexpected bonds had the power to shake up everything you thought you knew about life's direction.

Nicholas' keen perception didn't miss the fleeting change in Marc's demeanor—the way his eyes held a depth of emotion, a mixture of understanding and a hint of something more. It was like looking into a mirror that reflected his own intricate emotions back at him.

In that suspended moment, the air between them hummed with unspoken words and the electricity of shared vulnerability. It was a juncture where their feelings intersected, where the boundaries between friendship, attraction, and the complexities of life blurred into an indistinct mosaic.

Despite the subtle undercurrent of jealousy that Marc was grappling with, his gaze remained resolute and his smile genuine. There was a grace in the way he managed his emotions, an acknowledgment of the reality that their lives held room for multiple connections and diverse emotions.

'It's funny,' Marc began, his voice tinged with a wistful note. 'Our lives are a web of emotions, right? We're juggling dreams, desires, and the expectations others have for us. Sometimes, it's a thrilling dance, and other times, it's like walking on a tightrope.'

Nicholas nodded in agreement, a mix of intrigue and appreciation in his eyes. 'You've got that right. It's like we're all trying to find our balance in this digital age where we're constantly connected yet still navigating the depth of our feelings.'

Marc leaned back in his chair, the corners of his lips quirking into a rueful smile. 'And sometimes, those feelings can surprise us. Like this'—he motions his hands back and forth, not knowing the word to use—'we're building. It's unexpected, uncharted, and a little exhilarating.'

Nicholas' lips curled into a half-smile, a shared

understanding passing between them. 'Absolutely. It's a reminder that life is a mix of the planned and the spontaneous, the known and the unknown. And who knows where this might go?'

As their conversation flowed, each word was a steppingstone across the river of emotions they were navigating. In that café, amidst the aroma of coffee and the buzz of life around them, they were forging a unique bond—one that resonated with the modern complexity of human emotions and the potential for their lives to be reshaped by the unexpected connections they dared to embrace.

And so, in that coffee-scented corner of the world, their conversation continued—a dance of shared thoughts, unspoken yearnings, and the delicate balance of emotions that made their journey both thrilling and unpredictable.

Nicholas' gaze met Marc's, and he was struck by the depth of understanding he saw there. The connection they were forming was rooted in shared experiences of grappling with identity and authenticity. It was a connection that held the potential for something more profound than either of them had anticipated.

As the conversation continued, the vulnerability between them deepened. It was a journey of unraveling secrets, a medley of past experiences and present desires. And as the evening sun dipped below the horizon, casting a warm glow over their table, the subtle tension between them gave way to a moment of unspoken understanding.

At that moment, their eyes met, and Nicholas felt a pull that went beyond friendship. It was a moment of raw honesty that carried with it the potential to redefine their paths and rewrite their stories.

The café's ambiance faded into the background as their

hands brushed against each other, fingers entwining in a gentle dance of connection. And then, with a shared understanding and an act of courage that came from deep within, their lips met in a tender, intimate kiss—an unspoken promise of exploring the uncharted territory of their desires and discovering the truth within themselves.

And so, in the embrace of that moment, Nicholas and Marc embarked on a journey of self-discovery, navigating the intricate tapestry of their desires, past experiences, and shared connection. As their lips parted, the air around them seemed to crackle with electricity, an echo of the emotions coursing through their veins.

Their stories, once separate, were now intertwined, forming the chapters of a shared narrative that was both brave and unapologetic. And as they looked into each other's eyes, they understood that their journey had only just begun, with all its complexities, uncertainties, and the promise of finding their own truth in the midst of it all.

Chapter 5

Growing Bond

Weeks melted into days, and the serendipitous meeting between Nicholas and Marc morphed into a relationship. A relationship that was still teetering on a fence of friendship and deep romance. What had started as a brief connection had now grown into an unforeseen and deeply meaningful journey, albeit one that unfolded amidst the flashing caution lights and the symbolic police tape of their own apprehensions.

Their meetings at the café became more frequent, each interaction filled with laughter, shared stories, and an unspoken understanding. It was as if their souls recognized each other, and in each other's company, they found a refuge from the complexities of their lives.

One afternoon, as the sun cast a warm glow over the city, Nicholas found himself sitting across from Marc again. The hum of conversation and the aroma of coffee surrounded them, cocooning them in a world that felt entirely their own.

'Nicholas, there's something I need to ask you,' Marc began, his voice gentle.

Nicholas looked up, curious. 'Yes? What?'

Marc paused, his gaze locked onto Nicholas' with a friendly determination. 'All right, spill it. So, spill the beans. There's something on your mind, something you're still wrestling with, some apprehension. Tell me.' As he leaned toward Nicholas for support, illustrating that he wants some clarity.

The sincerity in Marc's approach resonated deeply with Nicholas. It felt like the universe had orchestrated this moment, bringing someone so empathetic and open-minded into his life.

Nicholas drew in a deep breath, his chest tightening with a mixture of trepidation and resolve. His heart thrummed against his ribcage as he nodded slowly, his eyes searching for understanding in Marc's gaze. 'There's something I've been carrying within me, something I've never shared with anyone before,' he confessed, his voice a fragile thread that seemed to hang in the air. 'I think I'm... bisexual.'

His words, once spoken, felt like a weight lifted from Nicholas' shoulders, yet their vulnerability hung heavily in the air. His gaze remained locked on Marc, a mix of anticipation and anxiety swirling within him. In those moments, he felt an overwhelming need for acceptance and understanding.

Marc's demeanor softened, a gentle smile playing on his lips. His eyes conveyed a sense of comfort and reassurance as they locked onto Nicholas', silently conveying his steadfast commitment to being there for him. 'I had a feeling something was on your mind,' Marc admitted with a gentle chuckle, his tone tinged with affection. 'Especially after our first, second, third, and to be honest, I have lost count of the number of times we have now met for our afternoon tête-à-tête.'

Nicholas' lips twitched in a ghost of a smile, relieved by Marc's lighthearted response. He appreciated the ease with which Marc could approach the topic, even with its weight. 'You caught that, huh?' he remarked, a mixture of self-consciousness and amusement in his voice.

Marc's grin widened, a playful glint in his eyes. 'I was hoping that something was up, since, well, you know, the kissing stuff,' he teased, his words accompanied by a mischievous wink.

A genuine laugh escaped Nicholas' lips, the tension he had been carrying since entering the café dissipating like morning mist under the sun's warmth. 'You've got a point there,' he conceded with a shake of his head, a soft chuckle lingering in his voice. 'But honestly, I've been grappling with this for a long time. Suppressing it, ignoring it, and just... pretending.'

Marc's expression softened even more, his eyes brimming with empathy. 'Nicholas, I can't even imagine how tough that must've been. To have to hold onto something like that, to feel like you had to keep a part of yourself hidden.'

Nicholas' shoulders eased as he exhaled a sigh, the relief of sharing his truth palpable. 'It's been a struggle,' he admitted, his voice heavy with the weight of years spent denying his own identity. 'And I think I've reached a point where I can't keep living inauthentically.'

Marc reached across the table, placing his hand on top of Nicholas' with a comforting squeeze. 'You're not alone in this journey. And no matter what, your feelings and your truth matter.'

Nicholas' eyes connected with Marc's, a sense of gratitude swelling inside him. 'Marc, I really appreciate you for being by my side, for lending an ear, for truly getting me. I can't deny this pull toward you, and it's not just that—I find myself irresistibly drawn to your smile, your face, and those beautiful eyes that seem to see right into me.'

Marc's smile held a warmth that reached his heart, his genuine pride for Nicholas evident in the way he looked at him. But then, his smile softened, and he leaned back in his chair, his expression thoughtful. 'I am so proud of you for finally being able to say the words,' he began, his voice carrying a depth of sincerity. 'But, Nicholas, where do you see me in this revelation?

I mean, I've been a part of your journey through this, right? How do I fit into all of this? Am I a part of your becoming?'

As Nicholas looked into Marc's eyes, a whirlwind of emotions swirled within him. The question Marc posed cut straight to the heart of the matter, forcing him to confront the complexities of his feelings. His connection with Marc had transcended the casual and entered a realm that was both exhilarating and uncharted. He hesitated, not out of doubt about his feelings, but because he wanted to articulate them in a way that did justice to their depth.

'You are absolutely a part of this,' Nicholas replied, his voice steady despite the whirlwind within. 'From the moment we met, you've been a source of understanding, acceptance, and support. Opening up to you about my feelings, about who I am—it's been liberating. And it's made me realize that this isn't just by chance. It's something I've come to yearn for and know that I want.'

Nicholas paused, his gaze never leaving Marc's. 'You've helped me find the courage to be honest with myself, and that's a gift I can't overlook. But beyond that, you've become someone who challenges me to see the world and myself in new ways. I think of you and our conversations as a safe haven, a place where I can be unapologetically myself.'

Marc's eyes held a mixture of surprise and warmth, his lips curving into a tender smile. 'Nicholas, thank you. But I also want you to know that while I've been here to support you, your journey is your own. I don't want to be the reason you make decisions or take steps that you might later regret. You deserve the space to explore your identity on your own terms.'

Nicholas gave a nod, really understanding what Marc was saying. 'Yeah, I get that, and I appreciate that you're giving me space to figure things out on my own. And about you, well, you're like a key character in my story. I can't see the whole plot yet, but I know you've already changed the story's direction in a big way.'

Marc's smile grew even warmer; his eyes locked onto Nicholas with intensity. 'You know, you've left your mark on my heart too. This, us, means a lot to me, and I'm here for you, regardless of which road you take. I'm all in, ready to be a part of whatever journey you decide to embark on.'

In that moment, as their words lingered in the air, Nicholas felt a sense of clarity amidst the uncertainty. Their meeting wasn't just a chance encounter, it was a meaningful and transformative chapter in his life. As they continued to navigate their feelings and experiences, Nicholas knew that he had a true partner in Marc—a partner who would be there through the highs and lows of his becoming.

'You're absolutely a part of my journey,' Nicholas said, his voice steady but infused with a hint of vulnerability. 'From the moment we met, there's been something about you that's drawn me in—a sense of authenticity, a willingness to listen, and a connection that's hard to define. When I'm around you, I feel like I can be myself without the need to put up any facades. And that's been crucial for me as I've come to terms with my own identity. I have felt comfortable with you from day one, and I attribute that to you and not others.'

Marc's gaze remained focused on Nicholas, his eyes reflecting a mix of emotions—curiosity, understanding, and a hint of something more. 'I'm glad to hear that,' he replied, his voice soft. 'But it also raises a lot of questions. I've seen how you've struggled, how you've been torn between your feelings and your commitment to Brooke.'

Nicholas nodded, his eyes dropping to his hands as he intertwined his fingers. 'It's been a constant battle within me,' he admitted. 'I love Brooke, I truly do. Our marriage meant something when we exchanged our vows. But as time has passed, I've realized that there's a part of me I've been ignoring, a part that's equally important.'

Marc's expression remained empathetic, his understanding evident in the way he listened. 'And where do I fit into that equation?' he asked gently. 'I don't want to be the reason for any difficult decisions you might have to make.'

Nicholas looked up, seeing him wholeheartedly. 'You're not the sole reason,' he said earnestly. 'But meeting you, connecting with you, it's shown me that I can't keep denying who I am. And while our connection has made me question my life's choices, I don't regret it. You've become a confidant; someone I can talk to openly about my feelings and fears. Someone that I have these feelings for, and they keep pulling me to you, back to you, in a way that I have never experienced before.'

Marc's lips curved into a soft smile, a mixture of emotions dancing in his eyes. 'I'm happy to be that person for you,' he said, his voice gentle albeit slightly nervous. 'But what does all of this mean for us? For you and me?'

Nicholas exhaled a slow breath, his gaze returning to the table as he contemplated his response. 'I don't have all the answers,' he admitted. 'But I know that I don't want to dismiss this. You've brought something into my life that I've been missing, a sense of authenticity and understanding. And I want to build something new with you, but I also need to deal with my present and my past.'

Marc nodded, his expression a blend of hope and caution. 'I appreciate your honesty,' he said quietly. 'But we also can't ignore the reality of your marriage. Brooke is a part of your life, and I don't want to cause any harm.'

Nicholas' fingers traced the rim of his coffee cup, his

thoughts spinning with the situation's complexities. 'You're right,' he acknowledged, his voice tinged with a mix of frustration and longing. 'This isn't a simple path to navigate. I don't want to hurt Brooke, and I don't want to hurt you either.'

Nicholas' thoughts swirled in a storm of contemplation as he mulled over the complexity of his emotions. He questioned if he was being fair to anyone involved, pondered the weight of his choices, and tried to envision the path ahead—a path that held uncertainty and the potential for happiness and heartache in equal measure. It was a crossroads that he couldn't ignore, a juncture that would undoubtedly shape the course of his life and the lives of those he cared about. Well fuck, he thought silently, I am just setting myself up for more rejection, but so far it has been great.

Nicholas' thoughts are drawn back as Marc reaches out, his hand covering Nicholas' briefly before pulling away. 'Nicholas, I want you to figure this out for yourself,' he said gently. 'I care about you and want you to find your own truth, even if it means taking the time you need.'

Nicholas looked up, meeting Marc's gaze with gratitude. 'Thank you. Your understanding means the world to me. I just hope that whatever happens, we can continue to be a part of each other's lives.'

Marc's smile transformed into a warm and comforting one. 'We're in this together,' he said, shifting his seating position to snuggle up against Nicholas. Nicholas responded by wrapping his arm around the curve of Marc's lower back, pulling him close. Marc rested his head on Nicholas' shoulder as the café bustled around them. Amidst the activity, there was a distinct intimacy between them, a sanctuary where openness was met with understanding and embrace. It was in those precious moments that the space between them seemed to melt away, leaving only the profound connection they were nurturing—a connection that had the potential to reshape their lives in ways they hadn't even imagined. Nicholas tenderly leaned in and pressed a soft kiss to Marc's parted lips. In a gentle voice, he whispered, 'Marc, you've completely reshaped how I perceive love.'

Chapter 6

Dinner, Dancing, and Ugh.

The café was a vibrant hub, buzzing with energy and warmth, where Nicholas and Marc found themselves enveloped in an ambiance of modern charm. The scent of rich coffee mingled with their laughter, weaving a tapestry of connection that felt fresh and exciting. Over recent months, their random encounters had blossomed into deliberate, meaningful interactions, laying the groundwork for a budding relationship that felt both thrilling and new.

Nicholas sipped his coffee, his eyes meeting Marc's with a mixture of nervousness and determination. The words he had been rehearsing danced on the tip of his tongue, and he knew it was time to take the next step. 'Marc,' he began, his voice steady despite the fluttering in his chest, 'I've been thinking... would you like to have dinner with me sometime?'

Marc's reaction was a delightful blend of astonishment and joy. With a bright smile, he responded, 'I'd love that!'

As they chatted about life in the bustling city, they shared their unique takes and experiences, finding common ground in their perspectives. Nicholas, leaning back, shared his admiration for the city's vibrant energy and diverse culture, while Marc agreed but also expressed his nostalgia for a simpler, quieter life.

Their conversation was a lively exchange of viewpoints and laughter, touching on everything from Central Park's serene beauty amidst urban chaos to the challenging winters in the city. They both acknowledged the enchanting allure of New York during the holiday season, reminiscing about its magical moments.

Nicholas leaned back in his chair, contemplating. 'You know, there's just a certain energy here that's unlike anywhere else. The diversity, the culture, the constant hustle and bustle, it's invigorating. I love how you can find anything and everything here. The food scene alone is a dream.'

Marc agreeing. 'You're right; the city is amazing, but sometimes, I miss the tranquility of a slower life. Like where I grew up. But I will say the gay life here is better.'

Nicholas smiled, appreciating Marc's perspective. 'I get that. The noise and the crowds can be overwhelming at times. The gay scene I cannot attest to, but it's a city of contrasts. Like Central Park, you have the serene parks right in the heart of all the chaos.'

Marc chuckled. 'True, Central Park is an oasis. And the city does have its charm, no doubt. But the cost of living, the rush-hour subway rides, and the winters here can be brutal.'

Nicholas laughed. 'Ah, the winters! They can be quite the test of endurance. We have the holiday season, and there's something magical about New York during that time.'

Marc's eyes softened with a hint of nostalgia. 'You're right; the city does have its moments of magic. And I can't deny it's given me some unforgettable experiences.'

As they continued to share their thoughts, it became evident that their love-hate relationship with New York was a testament to the city's complexity. It was a place that challenged them and rewarded them.

'Speaking of magic,' Marc began with a sly grin, 'where did you choose for us to go to dinner? Are you ready to show off your culinary expertise?'

Nicholas raised an eyebrow in mock suspicion. 'Are you doubting my choice of restaurants?'

Marc leaned in, his voice dripping with playful challenge. 'Well, I guess we'll have to find out, won't we?'

Their conversation shifted seamlessly from dinner expectations to shared interests, with a dash of playful banter thrown in. Marc's enthusiasm for literature was infectious, and Nicholas found himself captivated by the way Marc's eyes lit up when he talked about his favorite novels.

'You know,' Marc said thoughtfully, 'there's something truly magical about losing yourself in a good book, about getting lost in a world that's not your own.'

Nicholas nodded in agreement. 'Absolutely. It's like a temporary escape from reality, a chance to live multiple lives through the pages.'

Marc expelled, 'Whatever our souls are made of, his and mine are the same'.

Nicholas chimed in, 'Emily Bronte, Wuthering Heights, one of my favorites.' They both smile at one another with bashful expressions.

As their conversation flowed, Marc's expression turned thoughtful, his eyes locking onto Nicholas'. 'You know, it's strange how easily we connect. It's like we've known each other forever.'

Nicholas' heart skipped a beat, his own gaze locking onto Marc's. 'I've been thinking the same thing. It's almost like our paths were meant to cross.'

As the hours slipped away, their dialog remained vibrant and engaging, each revelation bringing them closer. The easy banter, the genuine interest in each other's lives—it all felt like the beginning of something significant.

The evening finally arrived, and Nicholas waited for Marc outside the café, his heart racing with a mixture of excitement and nerves. When Marc emerged, their eyes met, and Nicholas felt a rush of reassurance. 'Ready?' he asked with a smile.

Marc's grin was infectious. 'Absolutely.'

Marc had chosen a trendy new gay restaurant in the heart of the village for their dinner. As they settled into their seats, the atmosphere buzzed with energy and laughter. The menu was filled with delicious options, and as they perused it, Nicholas discovered that Marc was a vegetarian. 'Looks like you've got a preference for vegetarian dishes?' Nicholas remarked, a curious smile tugging at his lips.

Marc grinned playfully. 'Yeah, I've been on the vegetarian wagon for a while. It's not just about the food, it's also about all the other stuff. Plus, I've discovered some amazing dishes that have completely won me over.'

Nicholas smiled faintly, impressed by Marc's conscious choices. 'That's really good. I've never been a strict vegetarian myself, but I do appreciate a well-crafted meal.'

Their conversation flowed naturally as they shared their thoughts on food, their favorite dishes, and the experiences that had led them to their current preferences. It felt easy, as if they were uncovering yet another layer of commonality in their connection. The vibrant surroundings of the restaurant seemed to mirror the energy between them, each moment deepening the bond they were building.

Sitting across from each other, Nicholas and Marc found themselves delving into their pasts, sharing stories that painted vivid pictures of their upbringing.

Nicholas took a bite of his pasta, his gaze drifting as memories of his childhood resurfaced. 'I grew up in upstate New York, a small town surrounded by lush forests and rolling hills,' he began. 'I was the youngest of three, my parents working hard to provide for us. My mom was a teacher, always encouraging our education—'

Marc interjected with a smile, 'My dad was a history teacher.'

Nicholas continued, 'My dad worked long hours in a factory. It wasn't always easy, but they instilled in me the value of hard work and perseverance.'

'Nicholas, can I ask you a question?' Marc asked in a direct tone.

Nicholas replied with a quizzical 'yes.'

Nicholas' lips curved into a nostalgic smile. 'Funny story, actually. We both attended City University, and we met on the very first day of orientation. I remember being nervous and overwhelmed by the sheer size of the campus. I was lost, trying to find my way, and that's when Brooke approached me with a friendly smile. She offered to help me find my way around, and from that moment on, we were inseparable. We shared a lot of the same classes, studied together, and eventually, our friendship evolved into something deeper.'

Marc nodded, absorbing Nicholas' words. 'But do still love her.'

Nicholas chuckled softly. 'Do you really want to talk about my wife?'

Marc looked thoughtful, his gaze fixed on Nicholas. 'I think it's important, don't you? Understanding your feelings for her, it helps me understand you better.'

Nicholas sighed, running a hand through his hair. 'It's complicated, Marc. I mean, yes, I still care for her, but it's not the same as it used to be. Our relationship has changed so much, especially after everything that happened.'

Marc leaned in, his expression serious. 'And how do you feel about us, about me?'

Nicholas met Marc's gaze, his eyes filled with warmth. 'I am growing to care about you, Marc. And I want to see where this will go.'

Marc smiled, a genuine and affectionate grin. 'Good, because I feel the same.'

Nicholas looked at Marc with understanding in his eyes. 'I know, Marc. I've seen how conflicted you've been about all of this. And I'm grateful that you've been honest with me, even when it's been difficult.'

Marc nodded, his shoulders slightly slumped. 'Yeah, it's just... I never wanted to be the cause of someone else's pain.'

Nicholas reached out and gently squeezed Marc's hand. 'I get it, really, I do. But we can't change the past, and we've both made choices that have led us here. The important thing now is to figure out how we move forward.'

Marc offered a faint smile. 'Time will tell.'

As they sat together, their hands intertwined, they knew that navigating the complexities of their relationship wouldn't be easy, but they were determined to face it together.

As their conversation flowed, Marc felt compelled to change the conversation that he had started. He leaned back, a hint of vulnerability in his gaze. 'My childhood was quite different from yours,' he began. 'I grew up in a small town in Ohio, but it wasn't as idyllic as it might sound. It was a place where homophobia was rampant, and being different was not accepted.'

Nicholas' brows furrowed in empathy. 'I'm sorry you had to deal with all that.'

Marc shrugged his shoulders, his expression a mixture of sadness and strength. 'It's a part of who I am. I was an only child, my mother stayed at home, and as I said, my dad was a history teacher at the local high school. I loved school, but being different made me a target for bullying and abuse. It was tough, but it made me resilient.'

Nicholas reached across the table, placing his hand on Marc's, a gesture of support. 'I am so sorry.'

Marc's lips curled into a wistful smile. 'Thank you. It wasn't easy, but it shaped me into who I am today.'

Nicholas gave a nod, a smile of recognition passing between them. 'I get it now. Your background has played a big role in shaping the caring and empathetic person you are today.' Marc's gaze held a mix of emotions.

'I am sure this is why I've never been in a real relationship before,' he admitted, his voice tinged with vulnerability. 'I guess growing up in that environment made me wary of showing my true self to others.'

Nicholas' eyes softened, his heart going out to Marc. 'I'm glad you're relaxed enough to be yourself with me.'

Marc's smile held a touch of gratitude. 'Meeting you has been amazing. You've shown me there's more to love and connection than discontent and fear.'

Nicholas' grip on Marc's hand tightened, his eyes reflecting a mixture of gratitude and determination. 'You've shown me that embracing who you truly are is a journey worth taking, no matter the obstacles.' He leaned in, their lips meeting in a soft and electric connection, a spark igniting the space between them as their breaths intertwined.

The evening sun cast a warm glow on their faces, they continue to talk. They were building a connection that was rooted in mutual understanding, empathy, and a shared desire for authenticity. And as their conversation continued, they realized that they were on a journey of healing and growth, one that had the potential to lead them to a future they had only dreamed of.

After dinner, they decided to continue the night with a visit to a nearby club. The vibrant music and energetic crowd enveloped them as they stepped inside. The dim lighting and pulsating beats seemed to match the rhythm of their hearts, and Nicholas felt a surge of exhilaration as Marc took his hand, leading him to the dance floor.

They danced, their bodies moving in sync to the music, the distance between them gradually diminishing. The chemistry that had been simmering beneath the surface ignited, and as their bodies pressed closer, the world around them seemed to fade away. The connection between them deepened with every sensual movement, and Nicholas found himself lost in the intensity of the moment.

Surrounded by the pulsating music and the rhythm of the dance floor, their lips met in fervent kisses that conveyed a profound yearning. The taste of Marc's mouth was an enchanting blend of sensations, and as they separated, their breaths intermingling, Nicholas' heart raced with a potent mixture of feelings. He sensed the fervor not only in his chest but also in his pants. An undeniable sexual tension had ignited between them, unlike anything he had ever encountered. The allure was electric as he locked eyes with Marc, absorbing the sight of his soft lips, his snug T-shirt that lifted slightly above his jeans, revealing a trace of fine blond hair along a mesmerizing treasure trail. Temptation danced in his gaze, fixated on an alluring shape beneath Marc's denim. In response, Marc captured his attention, his grip on Nicholas' hand assertive as he drew him into a passionate embrace, their bodies melding with passion.

As they left the club, arm in arm, their steps light and their laughter mingling with the night air, their joy was palpable. But fate had other plans in store for them. As they turned a corner, Nicholas' heart skipped a beat when he saw a familiar face—

Brooke's cousin Nathan. In that moment, panic surged through him, and his mind raced with thoughts of how to explain their presence at the club.

Nathan's eyebrows raised in mild surprise, a playful smile on his lips. 'Well, well, what do we have here? Enjoying the night?'

Nicholas' mind spun, his heart pounding in his chest. Marc's reassuring presence by his side was a lifeline, and he took a deep breath, summoning the courage to respond.

'Hey, Nathan. Yes, I just decided to have a night out. This is my friend Marc.'

Nathan's gaze flickered between them and a knowing smirk curved his lips. 'Looks like a lot of fun,' he baited, his eyes twinkling impishly.

Nathan said, 'Get home safe.' As he continued down the street with his two friends.

In that moment, the weight of the situation crashed over Nicholas, and his chest tightened. Panic began to claw at the edges of his consciousness, threatening to overwhelm him. His breath quickened, and his thoughts spiraled as he struggled to control the surge of anxiety.

Sensing Nicholas' distress, Marc stepped closer, his voice calm and soothing. 'Hey, Nicholas, look at me. Breathe.'

Nicholas' eyes met Marc's, and in the midst of his panic, the familiarity of Marc's gaze anchored him. Marc's words became a lifeline, guiding him back to the present moment. Slowly, he took deep breaths, his focus shifting from the racing thoughts to the steady rhythm of his inhales and exhales.

Marc's hand found its way to Nicholas' back, offering gentle support. 'You're safe,' he reassured, his voice a soothing balm. 'Just keep breathing. You're not alone.'

As the minutes ticked by, the panic subsided, leaving behind a sense of vulnerability and relief. Nicholas' chest felt lighter, and he looked at Marc with a mixture of gratitude and embarrassment. 'Thank you,' he whispered, his voice carrying the weight of his emotions.

As they walked, the city's familiar sounds served as a backdrop to the quiet conversation between Marc and Nicholas. The tension from the recent panic attack was still palpable, yet their connection remained steadfast.

'You doing okay now?' Marc asked gently, his gaze fixed on the path ahead.

Nicholas nodded, his expression a mix of gratitude and vulnerability. 'Yeah, thank you. I'm sorry you had to see that.'

Marc's response was immediate, laced with sincerity. 'Nicholas, you don't have to apologize for how you feel. We all have our moments.'

Nicholas' lips curved into a small, appreciative smile. 'I'm lucky to have you by my side, Marc.'

They continued walking in companionable silence for a moment before Marc's curiosity got the better of him. 'Hey, what about the guy? Are you close with him?'

Nicholas' shoulders tensed slightly, a fleeting shadow crossing his eyes. 'Yeah, Nathan and I go way back, he's Brooke's cousin. He's been a good friend for a long time.'

Marc picked up on the hesitation and the slight fear in Nicholas' voice and decided not to press further. Instead, he changed the topic, seeking to lighten the mood. 'So, any other hidden talents or secrets I should know about?'

Nicholas chuckled softly, his shoulders relaxing. 'Well, besides my knack for awkward situations, I'm a pretty decent cook. And I can play the guitar, although I don't do it as much as I used to.'

Marc's eyes sparkled with curiosity. 'A cook and a musician? Impressive.'

Nicholas shrugged modestly. 'Just hobbies, really. What about you? Any hidden talents?'

Marc grinned playfully. 'Well, I have a knack for finding the juiciest gossip in town. Kidding, mostly.'

They reached Nicholas' doorstep, and he turned to face Marc with a soft smile. 'Thank you for walking me home. I know tonight was… unexpected.'

Marc returned the smile, his eyes warm. 'No need to thank me. I'm here for you.'

Nicholas' fingers brushed against Marc's arm in a gesture that spoke volumes of their growing connection. 'Goodnight, Marc.'

'Goodnight, Nicholas.'

Marc watched as Nicholas entered his building before turning to head back, his heart a mix of concern and affection for the man he was growing to care deeply about.

Given the situation that had unfolded, a wave of distress washed over Marc like a torrential downpour. Seeing Nicholas struggle with his panic attack had rattled him, igniting a flurry of emotions within himself. Doubt, concern, and a lingering unease swirled together in a tempest of feelings.

As Nicholas began to regain his composure with Marc's support, the aftermath left Marc questioning his own role and decisions. His mind was a canvas splashed with the hues of uncertainty. 'What am I doing?' he pondered, the weight of his thoughts nearly audible. The path they were treading was both exhilarating and treacherous, lined with unforeseen twists and turns. Marc's heart was undoubtedly drawn to Nicholas, but the complications of their connection loomed large.

In that moment, as the city bustled around them, Marc's inner dialog echoed with introspection. He recognized that he was charting unexplored territory, venturing into a realm where emotions ran deep and boundaries blurred. The fragility of Nicholas' mental state had laid bare the complexity of their situation, and Marc couldn't help but wonder if he was capable of providing the support Nicholas truly needed.

Caught between his feelings for Nicholas and the weight of their circumstances, Marc's internal struggle intensified. He cared deeply for this man who had unexpectedly entered his life, igniting a spark that had grown into something far more profound. Yet, the potential pitfalls and challenges that accompanied their connection loomed large. Marc found himself grappling with the intricacies of his emotions, weighing his desires against the realities of the situation.

As he walked away from the scene, a cloud of uncertainty lingered over him. Marc's heart felt like a puzzle with missing pieces, a beautiful and intricate enigma that he was still attempting to decipher. While his affection for Nicholas was undeniable, the gravity of the path they were traversing weighed heavily on him. The question of whether he was making the right choices, not just for himself but for Nicholas too, gnawed at him.

In the midst of the city's chaos, Marc's thoughts churned like a tempestuous sea. He knew that the road ahead was fraught with challenges, but his heart couldn't dismiss the undeniable connection he shared with Nicholas. As he navigated his way through the labyrinth of emotions, one thing remained clear: the journey they were on was far from easy, but it was a journey he wants to take; but at this point, he had clear hesitation.

Chapter 7

Calm Days in the Library

The library was a realm of quiet comedy, its shelves a sitcom of sagas and tales. Marc, the unofficial librarian-jester, held court at the reference desk, tapping out a whimsical tune on the keyboard as he navigated the literary circus for patrons. The quirky events of the past months with Nicholas prickled his thoughts, prompting a brief interlude in their comedic capers while hiding the truth.

Meanwhile, Marc's phone buzzed softly on the desk, notifications from texts he had received from Nicholas:

Nicholas: *Hey, Marc, I hope you're doing okay. I wanted to reach out and apologize again for what happened the other night. I truly didn't mean for things to spiral like that.* 😔

Nicholas: *I know it must have been awkward and uncomfortable, and I'm really sorry for any stress I caused. I value you a lot and don't want it to be tainted by that incident.*

Nicholas: *If you're up for it, can we meet and talk? Maybe clear the air?*

Nicholas: *I am just... unsure... I feel like an interloper.*

Marc: *Hey, Nicholas, you're not... what happened had nothing to do with you.*

Marc: *I understand that the other night was unexpected for both of us. It caught me off guard, but I get that things can get complicated sometimes.*

Marc: *We'll figure this out, okay?*

Nicholas: *Thank you, Marc. Your understanding means a lot to me, and I don't want anything to get in the way.* 😊

Nicholas: *Let's meet at the café.*

Nicholas: *Also, I'm sorry again for any distress I caused. I promise to explain everything and hopefully clear up any confusion.*

Marc: *Meeting at the café is fine.*

Marc: *Just let me know when you're available.*

Nicholas: *How about tomorrow evening? Around seven P.M.? Does that work for you?*

Marc: *Tomorrow at seven P.M. works.*

Nicholas: *Looking forward to it, Marc. Thank you for being understanding and giving me a chance. See you tomorrow.*

Marc appreciated Nicholas' efforts, but he really needed some space to process his emotions. He knew their feelings were genuine, but the events at the club had shaken him, leaving him grappling with his own vulnerabilities and insecurities. He found solace in the library's quiet, surrounded by the world of books that had always been his sanctuary. Seeing a copy of *Dorian Grey* lying on a cart, he thought, 'Keep love in your heart. A life without it is like a sunless garden when the flowers are dead.' This was a reminder that finding love is an integral part of life.

Marc's attention was drawn to a tall, slender blonde woman who approached the reference desk as the afternoon sun cast a warm glow through the library windows. Her eyes held a curious spark as she leaned forward, her voice carrying a note of enthusiasm. 'Hi, I'm looking for recommendations on current trends in young adult authors.'

'I am working on a marketing campaign to try to encourage

more reading with these video kids we have created,' she said passionately and enthusiastically.

Marc's smile was genuine as he leaned in, eager to share his passion for literature. 'Of course! Young adult fiction still exists. Are you interested in a specific theme, topic, or author?'

The woman's eyes brightened; her enthusiasm was contagious. 'I'm open to anything that has a spread of popularism right now. I want to explore some fresh voices and perspectives.'

Marc nodded, his fingers flying over the keyboard as he pulled up a list of popular young adult authors and their latest releases. As he began to discuss various titles and themes, their conversation flowed seamlessly, and Marc was reminded of the joy he found in connecting with others through the world of books.

'Here are some titles on bullying, the earth, diverse families, and LGTBQ+... you can 'literally' take your pick,' Marc expressed with great passion.

The lady, with a great smile, said, 'I like them all. I appreciate your help. Marc, is it?'

Marc smiled. 'Yes, it is.'

After a thoughtful discussion, the woman selected several books to check out. She reached into her bag, her movements confident and graceful, before pausing with a frown. 'I can't find my library card. Could you look me up by name?'

'Of course,' Marc replied, his fingers poised over the keyboard. 'May I have your last name, please?'

The woman's response was automatic, a casual statement that struck Marc like a lightning bolt. 'Jameson. Brooke Jameson.'

Time seemed to stand still for Marc as he processed the name. Brooke Jameson—the name that belonged to Nicholas' wife. His heart raced as he fought to conceal his emotions, his gaze fixed on the woman's face. It was then that he noticed her wallet resting on the counter, a wallet that she had retrieved to search for her library card.

As she opened the wallet, Marc's eyes caught a glimpse of a photograph tucked inside. A photograph of Nicholas. In that moment, everything seemed to converge—the woman's identity, the realization of her connection to Nicholas, and the weight of the secrets that had been kept.

Marc's hands felt numb as he continued to type, searching for Brooke Jameson's account. His mind raced, thoughts and emotions swirling like a tempest. He wanted to look away, to process what he had discovered, but he couldn't tear his gaze from the photograph that had unexpectedly shattered his sense of calm.

As the account details appeared on the screen, Marc's voice was steady, betraying none of his inner turmoil. 'I've found your account, Ms. Jameson. You're all set to check out these books.'

The woman's gratitude was genuine as she thanked Marc and gathered her belongings. Marc watched her walk away, his mind a whirlwind of thoughts and questions. The truth he had uncovered was a heavy burden to carry, and he felt the weight of his emotions threatening to spill over.

As the library continued to buzz with activity around him, Marc's gaze remained fixed on the spot where Brooke Jameson had stood. The sense of calm he had sought seemed like a distant memory, replaced by the storm of emotions that raged within him. And in the midst of it all, one question echoed louder than the rest: what did this revelation mean for his relationship with Nicholas?

Marc immediately texted Nicholas:

Marc: *I think your wife was just here?*
Buzz...
Nicholas: *What? Are you serious?*
Marc: *Yeah, I saw her at the library. She was asking about current young adult authors and mentioned her name is Brooke Jameson.*
Nicholas: *Oh my God, that's her.*
Nicholas: *Are you okay? Do you want to talk about it?*
Marc: *I don't even know where to start. This is so unexpected.*
Nicholas: *Of course, but she doesn't know anything. She didn't know who you were.*
Marc: *I need some time. We shouldn't meet tomorrow.*
Nicholas: *No, please. I need to see you. She did not suspect anything.*
Marc: *Maybe not, but I now have a face with the name. I feel bad. I need a minute. I will text you in the morning.*
Nicholas: *Marc, it will be all right, I will make it all right. Please see me tomorrow...*
Nicholas: *Marc?*

Marc's emotions were a whirlwind of confusion and concern. He couldn't believe the unexpected turn of events and how it was impacting both Nicholas and himself. The revelation that Brooke had shown up at the library left Marc feeling a mix of sympathy and unease.

As Nicholas expressed his desperation to see Marc the next day, Marc's heart ached with empathy. He understood Nicholas' need for comfort and reassurance, but at the same time, Marc needed a moment to process everything that had just happened. He felt a sense of guilt for having seen Brooke and having this newfound knowledge.

Nicholas' persistence in wanting to meet again tugged at Marc's heartstrings, but he knew he needed to sort through his own feelings before they could move forward. Marc's response conveyed his need for space, his struggle with the unexpected situation, and his hope that things could be resolved.

As he typed his final message, Marc's fingers hovered over the keypad, his heart heavy with conflicting emotions. He cared deeply for Nicholas and wanted to be there for him, but he also needed time to come to terms with the reality of the situation. The uncertainty of what lay ahead weighed on Marc's mind, leaving him feeling torn between his connection with Nicholas and the complexities of the path they were navigating.

Marc: *I will text in the morning.*

Chapter 8

Nicholas' Home with Brooke

After receiving the message that Marc encountered Brooke in the library, Nicholas was gripped by a swirling mix of emotions, a maelstrom of fear and anxiety. It was as if his world had suddenly tilted on its axis, and he was struggling to find his footing. Brooke now not more than two feet away from him... he could feel the light headedness swooning inside.

Nicholas couldn't help but replay the encounter at the library in his mind, imagining each detail like a vivid snapshot of impending disaster. Brooke's cheerful voice as she talked about her day, her enthusiasm about the child's author account she was working on. It all felt like a relentless drumbeat of dread.

He had been so close to losing control of the situation. If Brooke had lingered just a little longer, if she had any idea who Marc was, their delicate house of cards would have crumbled. The thought sent a chill down Nicholas' spine.

The fear of being caught was not just about the potential consequences of his actions, but also the betrayal it would mean for Brooke, the person he had promised to cherish and protect. He had always been the stable one in their relationship, the dependable partner. The guilt of betraying her trust weighed heavily on him, a gnawing sensation in the pit of his stomach.

Yet, in the midst of this turmoil, there was the undeniable truth of his feelings for Marc. Their connection was a lifeline in a world that had grown increasingly complex and confusing. Nicholas had never imagined he would even have feelings for a man, and certainly not while married to Brooke. The fear of losing Marc, of extinguishing the spark of something beautiful that had ignited between them, was equally paralyzing.

As he anxiously awaited Marc's response, to his final text, knowing that he needed to text back:

Marc: *I will text in the morning.*

Nicholas couldn't help but wonder how he had arrived at this point in his life. It was a place of profound contradiction where love and fear, desire and guilt, commitment and betrayal all converged into an emotional frenzy. The tightrope he was walking seemed impossibly thin, and he was acutely aware that one wrong step could send everything crashing down around him. As he waited to respond to Marc, the fear of losing him gnawed at Nicholas' heart. The mere thought of Marc walking away sent waves of panic through him.

He anxiously checked his phone, hoping for Marc's response, yearning for reassurance that they could navigate this storm together. But with every passing minute of silence, the fear that he might lose the man he had fallen for intensified, threatening to drown him in a sea of uncertainty and regret.

Nicholas sat on the sofa, his heart pounding in his chest as he stared at his phone. The texts from Marc were a lifeline he desperately needed, but with Brooke right there, he felt trapped in a web of lies and deceit. He couldn't risk her finding out about his secret relationship with Marc, yet he longed to respond to those messages, to let Marc know that he was okay and that they needed to talk.

Brooke, unaware of the turmoil within Nicholas, chattered on about her day.

'I had such an amazing day; I love this new account I am working on.' She looked at Nicholas for some form of responses.

Nicholas, still preoccupied with the recent encounter at the library, looked up, his expression distant. 'Oh, really? What is it about? I know you told me, but I forgot.'

Brooke's excitement waned as she registered Nicholas' distracted demeanor. She sighed softly, disappointment flickering across her features. 'Nick, we've been over this countless times in the past few weeks. It's about the Read Campaign. Remember? It's a significant project for me.'

Nicholas blinked, trying to focus on her words. 'I'm sorry,' he mumbled, his voice distant. 'There's just been a lot going on at work, and I guess my mind's been elsewhere.'

Brooke's expression softened with understanding, and she reached out to gently squeeze his hand. 'I know things have been stressful for you lately. But it's important for us to make time for each other, too. We can't let work consume our lives.'

Nicholas managed a weak smile, touched by her understanding. 'You're right, Brooke. I promise I'll be more present. Tell me more about this account. What makes it so special?'

As Brooke launched into an animated explanation of her work, Nicholas tried to push aside the whirlwind of emotions and worries that had plagued him since the library encounter. For now, he had to be the attentive and caring husband Brooke believed him to be, even as his heart continued to race with fear and longing for Marc.

'You won't believe it, Nick,' she said excitedly. 'I met the most wonderful guy at the library today. He was so helpful, and he even recommended some new children's authors for the Read Campaign. I think his name was Marc or Mike... no it was Marc.'

As Brooke continued to recount her encounter with Marc at the library, Nicholas felt like he was teetering on the edge of a precipice, one wrong move away from falling into a chasm of deception and exposure. He listened to her words, each one like a dagger slicing through his facade of normalcy.

'Nick, you should have seen him,' Brooke gushed, oblivious to the turmoil within her husband. 'He was so charming and knowledgeable. It's amazing how you can meet the most interesting people in the most unexpected places.'

Nicholas forced himself to nod and offer the occasional word of encouragement, all the while his thoughts spiraled into a whirl of anxiety. He was acutely aware of the weight of his wedding ring on his finger, a symbol of the life he had built with Brooke, and yet it felt like a shackle, a constant reminder of the secret he was harboring.

Questions and fears plagued him: What had Marc told Brooke about their meeting? Would she mention it again, probe deeper into her conversation with this 'charming' man? And what if she somehow discovered the truth? The thought of his carefully constructed world unraveling sent shivers down his spine.

Nicholas longed to reach for his phone, to send a message to Marc, to reassure himself that their connection remained intact. But he couldn't risk it, not with Brooke right there, her eyes filled with enthusiasm for her new acquaintance.

As the evening wore on, Nicholas felt the walls of his own home closing in on him. He had to maintain this disguise, keep up the charade of a loving husband, all while his heart ached for Marc, and the fear of being discovered gnawed at him. The weight of his secrets was becoming unbearable, and the chasm between the life he had and the life he desired seemed insurmountable.

'Nick, I have had enough, are you there? What is going on?' expressed Brooke.

Nicholas nodded, his anxiety mounting. 'Yeah, it's just a lot of deadlines and projects piling up. You know how it goes.'

She placed a comforting hand on his shoulder. 'Well, don't work yourself too hard. Maybe a nice dinner will help you relax. Any preferences?'

Nicholas was torn. He desperately wanted to text Marc, but he couldn't do it with Brooke right there. He had to keep up the facade. 'I trust your judgment, Brooke. Surprise me.'

She smiled warmly. 'All right, I'll whip up something. Just hang tight.'

As Brooke headed into the kitchen, Nicholas seized the opportunity to check his phone again. He typed out a message to Marc, fingers trembling with anxiety:

Nicholas: *Marc, I'm so sorry that you had to meet Brooke this way and I know it was a shock. I never meant for you to be put in that situation. Please, let's talk.*

The minutes dragged on, and Nicholas felt like he was suffocating under the weight of his secret. No response!

Nicholas' heart pounded as he anxiously awaited a reply from Marc. With every passing second, the silence grew heavier, a palpable tension that seemed to constrict his chest. He couldn't shake the feeling of being caught in a trap of his own making, his desperation and guilt intensifying with each unresponsive moment.

As he stared at the screen, his mind raced through various scenarios: What if Marc was too upset to respond? What if he decided that this unexpected revelation was too much to bear? The fear of losing the connection he had forged with Marc, a connection that had come to mean the world to him, clawed at his insides.

Nicholas knew he had put Marc in an incredibly difficult position, and he berated himself for it. He had introduced Marc to his world without warning, unknowingly setting their paths to collide, and Brooke, who remained blissfully unaware of the turmoil beneath her husband's coverup.

Tears welled up in Nicholas' eyes as he contemplated the possibility of Marc walking away from him. The thought of losing the person who had come to represent authenticity, acceptance, and love in his life was almost unbearable. And yet, he understood that Marc deserved better than the chaotic existence Nicholas was offering.

With each passing second, Nicholas' anxiety grew, and he couldn't shake the feeling that he was teetering on the precipice of a life-altering decision. It was a moment of reckoning, one where he would have to confront not only his own desires but also the consequences of his actions.

Desperation and longing filled him as he continued to wait for a response, his phone a lifeline to the man who had come to mean so much to him. The uncertainty of Marc's reaction hung over him like a storm cloud, and Nicholas couldn't help but wonder if this was the beginning of the end.

When Brooke finally called him to the dinner table, Nicholas yelled, 'Be there in a minute. Let me wash up.' He went to the restroom and washed his face to dry his eyes and tried to make himself a little more presentable.

He forced himself to eat, even though his stomach was in knots. He kept glancing at his phone, hoping for a reply from Marc, but it remained silent.

After dinner, Brooke suggested they watch a movie together, but Nicholas couldn't concentrate on anything other than his phone. Brooke, now tired, said, 'Okay, I'm done, I'm going to bed, are you coming?'

Nicholas said, 'No, I will finish the movie and head back soon.' As she headed to bed, she gave him a gentle kiss on the cheek.

'Sleep well, Nick. You look like you could use it.'

Alone in the living room, Nicholas returned to his phone, desperately trying to reach Marc:

Nicholas: *Marc, I can't stop thinking about how you looked after seeing her. I'm terrified of losing you because of her. Please, I need you to understand.*

Nicholas: *Marc, I get that you might be angry. Hell, I'm angry at myself. But we can't just let this tear us apart. I need you in my life.*

Nicholas: *Marc, the thought of not having you terrifies me. You've become such an important part of my life, and I can't lose you now. Please, can we meet tonight?*

Nicholas: *Marc, I care so much about you. I can't lose you over this. I'm willing to do whatever it takes to make this right between us. Please, talk to me.*

Nicholas sits there waiting for a response, but nothing.

Chapter 9

Breaking Point

The morning light filtered through the curtains, casting a soft glow in Marc's room. He woke up with a heavy feeling in his chest, the events of the previous day still fresh in his mind. The sight of his phone on the bedside table reminded him of the unopened text messages from Nicholas.

Marc's tiredness was evident in the dark circles under his eyes, and his disheveled appearance reflected a restless night of tossing and turning. He had spent hours replaying the encounter with Brooke in his mind, trying to make sense of the situation and the impact it had on him. The lack of sleep only seemed to intensify his emotional turmoil.

He reached for his phone, hesitating for a moment before unlocking it. The notifications from Nicholas were still there, a reminder of the urgency. Marc knew he needed to respond, but as he said out loud, 'Fuck! What am I going to do? It's time to do adulting!'

A message posted up, then two, then three, then four, then five. Marc shook his head slightly due to the sensory overload.

Nicholas: *Marc, I'm so sorry that you had to meet Brooke this way and I know it was a shock. I never meant for you to be put in that situation. Please, let's talk.*

Nicholas: *Marc, I can't stop thinking about how you looked* *after seeing her. I'm terrified of losing you because of her. Please, I need you to understand.*

Nicholas: *Marc, I get that you might be angry. Hell, I'm angry at myself. But we can't just let this tear us apart. I need you in my life.*

Nicholas: *Marc, the thought of not having you terrifies me. You've become such an important part of my life, and I can't lose you now. Please, can we meet tonight?*

Nicholas: *Marc, I care so much about you. I can't lose you over this. I'm willing to do whatever it takes to make this right between us. Please, talk to me.*

Marc felt a tumultuous mix of emotions after reading Nicholas' messages. On one hand, he was hurt and angered by the unexpected encounter with Brooke at the library. He felt exposed, as if he had stumbled into a situation far more complex than he had ever imagined.

At the same time, Marc couldn't ignore the genuine remorse and fear in Nicholas' messages. He knew that Nicholas had become an important part of his life too, and the thought of losing him was painful. Marc was torn between his anger and his deepening feelings for Nicholas.

As he sat there, staring at his phone, he realized that he needed time to sort through his emotions and thoughts. He wasn't sure if meeting Nicholas today was the right decision, but he knew that he couldn't ignore the situation forever. The conflict within him was a storm of emotions, and he needed to find a way to navigate it.

Taking a deep breath, Marc typed out a message, his fingers pausing over the keys as he carefully chose his words. He wanted to convey his feelings honestly and openly, while also being mindful of Nicholas' own emotions and concerns.

Marc: *'Hey Nicholas,'* he began, his hands shaking ever so lightly as his nerves shivered through his body into his arms and hand.

As he hit send, Marc felt a mix of relief and apprehension. He knew that the conversation ahead wouldn't be easy, but he also recognized the importance of being honest with both him and Nicholas. The weight of the situation was still heavy on his shoulders, but he was determined to navigate it with integrity and compassion, both for himself and for Nicholas.

As Marc sat in his quiet apartment, his mind was a whirlwind of conflicting emotions. The events of the past few days had stirred up a storm of thoughts and questions, and he found himself grappling with the complexity of his feelings for Nicholas and the situation with Brooke.

The question that loomed largest in his mind was whether Nicholas would leave Brooke for him. Marc had never imagined himself being part of something that could potentially break apart a marriage. He understood the intricacies of long-term relationships, the history, the shared moments, and the commitment. But at the same time, he couldn't deny the intensity of his connection with Nicholas and the undeniable pull he felt toward him.

As he replayed their interactions, their conversations, and the moments they had shared, Marc realized how deeply he had grown to care for Nicholas. The tenderness in his gestures, the warmth in his words, and the raw vulnerability they had shared—it was a kind of intimacy that Marc had never experienced before. And he couldn't ignore the fact that Nicholas seemed to reciprocate those feelings.

Yet, with each thought of Nicholas, there was an

undercurrent of guilt. He questioned whether he was allowing his own desires to cloud his judgment, and whether he was becoming a catalyst for the potential end of a marriage. The idea of being the cause of heartbreak and upheaval weighed heavily on him, and he felt a sense of responsibility that he hadn't anticipated.

Marc's internal conflict was further intensified by the realization that he had already played a role in the recent events. Brooke's unexpected appearance at the library had been a direct result of their connection, and Marc couldn't shake the feeling that he was already causing disruption in her life.

He also questioned his own motivations. Was he pursuing this connection with Nicholas out of a genuine emotional bond? Or was he simply drawn to the thrill of something new and exciting? He knew he needed to be honest with himself and with Nicholas about his intentions, even if it meant facing uncomfortable truths.

The hours ticked by, and Marc's mind continued to churn. He knew that he couldn't keep avoiding the inevitable conversation with Nicholas. He needed to address their feelings, their connection, and the complexities of their situations.

As he continued, Marc felt a mix of determination and trepidation. He continued typing out the message to Nicholas, his fingers moving slowly as he carefully chose his words. He wanted to express the depth of his emotions while also acknowledging the gravity of the situation.

Marc: *I hope you're okay. I've been thinking about everything and trying to come to terms with having our situation slapped into my face. I need you to know that I care about you and want to be there for you. I also can't ignore the fact that there are complexities involved, and I don't want to be the cause of any* *pain or hurt. We need to have an honest conversation about where we stand and what this means for both of us.*

Marc: *But I also need a little more time to sort through this. It's not easy for me, and I hope you understand that.*

As he hit send, Marc's heart raced. He knew that whatever lay ahead, it wouldn't be easy. But he was determined to confront the conflict head-on, to navigate the storm of emotions with integrity and empathy, and to ultimately make the choices that were right for both him and Nicholas, no matter how challenging they might be.

As Marc stared at his phone, he saw the bubbles and three dots rise, then disappear, what seemed like an eternity they returned, then they leave... Marc's heart raced.

Nicholas' response came after a few moments, and Marc's heart sank as he read the message:

Nicholas: *Marc, I understand that this is complicated, and I don't want to rush you into anything. But please know that my feelings for you are real, and I can't bear the thought of losing you. I know that Brooke's appearance was unexpected, but it doesn't change how I feel about you. Can we please meet today to talk? I need to see you, to understand where we stand.*

Marc's eyes lingered on the screen for a moment, his chest tight with conflicting emotions. He felt a wave of guilt wash over him as he recognized the depth of pain in Nicholas' words. It was clear that his hesitation was hurting Nicholas, and Marc struggled with the weight of that realization.

Taking a deep breath, Marc began typing his response:

Marc: *Nicholas, I want you to know that I care about you* *too, and I appreciate your understanding. This isn't easy for me either, and I'm trying to navigate my feelings and the situation as honestly as I can. I do think we need to talk, and I'm willing to meet today. Can you come over to my apartment this afternoon?*

Within what appears to be less than a nanosecond, Nicholas responded:

Nicholas: *Yes, I will be there around three p.m.* ♡
Marc: *Okay.*

After sending the message, Marc put down his phone and leaned back in his chair. He couldn't shake the feeling of unease that had settled in his chest. He knew that meeting today was the right thing to do, that they needed to address the conflict and uncertainty between them. But he also knew that it wouldn't be an easy conversation, and the potential outcomes weighed heavily on his mind.

As the hours passed, Marc found himself alternating between moments of anticipation and anxiety. He replayed their interactions, their shared conversations, and the intimate moments they had experienced. He couldn't deny the depth of his feelings for Nicholas, but he also couldn't ignore the complexity of the situation.

In the midst of his anxiety and confusion, Marc considered the complexities of his relationship with Nicholas. Despite the shock of meeting Brooke, he couldn't deny the genuine feelings he had developed over the weeks they had spent together.

As he mulled over the situation, he realized that life was rarely black and white. Sometimes, it was filled with shades of gray, and he couldn't ignore the fact that his bond with Nicholas had brought happiness and authenticity into his life. He understood that Nicholas was trapped in a difficult marriage, and their connection had been a lifeline. However, after the shock of the situation had left him reeling, and he grappled with the difficult decision of whether to continue his relationship with Nicholas or to bring it to an end.

Marc knew he couldn't ignore the gravity of the situation. Meeting Brooke had shattered the illusion of their secret relationship. It had become painfully clear that their affair was built on a foundation of deception, and this troubled Marc deeply.

In the hours that followed, Marc often found himself in a state of inner turmoil. He questioned the authenticity of their bond and whether he could ever fully be trusted again. The fear of being caught and the guilt of being the 'other man' weighed heavily on his conscience.

While part of Marc longed to confront Nicholas and demand answers, another part of him recognized the complexity of their situation. He knew that ending the relationship would not be easy. They had shared intimate moments, forged a deep connection, and had become an integral part of each other's lives.

Instead of immediately texting Nicholas and making a rash decision, Marc chose to keep his thoughts to himself for a while. He believed that he needed time to gain clarity, to sort through his feelings, and to weigh the pros and cons of continuing or ending their relationship.

Marc grappled with the fear of hurting Nicholas, the allure of their connection, and the turmoil within his own heart. He knew that the decision he made, whether to continue or end the affair, would have profound consequences for both. 'But, come on what am I doing?' Marc asked himself out loud. He grabbed his face with his hands and screamed, 'aaaah!'

This small gesture brought him back to reality just enough to think with a little more clarity. As he grappled with the shock and confusion, Marc found himself standing at a crossroads in his relationship. While he was acutely aware of the deception and the challenges they faced, Marc couldn't deny the profound impact Nicholas had on his life.

Marc couldn't shake the feeling that Nicholas had become an integral part of his existence. Their connection, both emotional and physical, had brought a sense of completeness that Marc had never experienced before. He found himself longing for Nicholas' presence, his voice, and the warmth of his touch.

Marc recognized that ending the relationship would be a heart-wrenching decision. He couldn't ignore the fact that Nicholas had become a confidant, a source of support, and a wellspring of affection in his life. The connection they shared felt genuine, and despite the deception, Marc couldn't easily sever the bond they had formed.

As he lay on his sofa staring into space, and contemplating the future, Marc realized that the choice to keep Nicholas in his life wasn't just about their secret romance. It was about acknowledging the depth of their connection and the genuine affection they felt for each other. It was about embracing the joy, passion, and comfort that Nicholas brought into his life.

While the fear of being discovered still lingered in Marc's mind, he couldn't ignore the overwhelming desire to keep Nicholas close. He knew that their relationship was far from conventional, and it came with its own set of challenges and risks. However, Marc couldn't deny the significance of what they shared.

Marc's decision weighed heavily on his mind as he sat in his dimly lit apartment, anxiously staring at his phone to watch the time.

As the minutes turned into hours, Marc found himself replaying their journey together. The stolen moments, the shared laughter, the intimate conversations, and the electrifying chemistry—they all flashed vividly before his eyes. It was undeniable that Nicholas had become an irreplaceable presence in his life.

Despite the deception, Marc couldn't ignore the depth of their affair. Nicholas had not only been his secret lover but also a confidant, a source of emotional support, and an unexpected muse for his creative endeavors. Marc realized that their relationship had breathed new life into him, inspiring his work and rekindling his passion for literature.

In the silence of his apartment, Marc's apprehension began to wane, replaced by a longing to hear Nicholas' voice, to understand the turmoil that had led them to this point. He knew they needed to talk, to lay their feelings bare, and to confront the tangled web of secrets and desires they had woven.

Uncertain of what to do next, Marc decided to wait for Nicholas. He believed in the power of them, in the authenticity of the emotions they shared. Marc knew that they couldn't simply brush this under the rug and move on. They needed to face the truth, even if it meant confronting the complexities of their secret love affair.

As he sat in the dimness of his apartment, Marc held onto a glimmer of hope. He hoped that their conversation, whenever it happened, would provide clarity, closure, or perhaps even a way forward. Marc understood that their relationship was far from conventional, but it had become an undeniable part of his life—one he wasn't quite ready to let go of.

So, he waited, ready to listen, to understand, and to see what the conversation with Nicholas would bring. It was a daunting prospect, but it was a path Marc felt compelled to tread, for better or for worse.

BUZZ! Marc sprang to his feet. Heart racing! 'Oh god, he is here.'

Chapter 10

Sunday Afternoon Tears

As Marc slowly walked to the door and lifted the intercom receiver, a whirlwind of emotions and thoughts raced through his mind. He was frozen in that moment, torn between conflicting feelings and uncertainties. His heart ached with a deep longing for Nicholas. But now, as he stood at the door, he faced the harsh reality of their situation. This single buzz would change everything.

Marc grappled with a difficult decision in that frozen moment by the intercom. Should he open the door, allowing Nicholas into the apartment, or should he step back, protecting himself? It was a moment of profound inner conflict, and the weight of his choice hung heavily in the air. He presses. *BUZZ!*

The sun cast long shadows in the late afternoon, and as Nicholas arrived in Marc's apartment, the lack of sleep was etched upon his face. His eyes, once bright and full of life, were now heavy-lidded and worn from a night spent wrestling with his conscience. He knew that today was the day he had to confront the chaos that had engulfed his life.

Marc, standing in the center of the living room, was a picture of anxiety. His flushed face and trembling hands betrayed the turmoil that had taken residence within him. The memory of encountering Brooke at the library still haunted him, her cheerful demeanor a stark contrast to the secret life Nicholas was leading. Silence enveloped them like a heavy blanket, suffocating and inescapable. The unspoken words hung in the air, thick with tension, as if daring one of them to break the stillness. Nicholas couldn't bear the weight of their unspoken emotions any longer, and he took a tentative step toward Marc.

'Marc,' he began, his voice barely rising above a whisper, 'I can't stop thinking about what happened. I can't bear to see you hurt like this.'

Marc, his anxiety giving way to profound sadness, blinked back tears. 'Nicholas,' he replied, his voice fragile but determined, 'I never signed up for this. I never wanted to be the secret in your life. I deserve more than that.'

The tears flowed freely, their shared vulnerability breaking down the barriers they had carefully constructed. A long pause enveloped them as they stood there mesmerized by each other's faces.

Marc finally shattered the silence, his voice trembling but resolute.

'No, Nicholas,' he said, his voice quivering, 'we can't keep doing this.'

Nicholas' fear illustrated reality, his tears mirroring Marc's. 'No,' he whispered, guilt and longing heavy in his voice, 'I just need time to sort things out with Brooke; I will leave her. I want you.'

Marc, who had heard similar promises before, couldn't immediately trust Nicholas' words. He had felt the depth of their connection, but he also knew the complexities of their situation. 'Oh, okay,' he retorted, bitterness lacing his tone, 'like every married man ever said.'

Desperate to convey the sincerity of his intentions, Nicholas grabbed Marc's hand and held it tightly. 'No, Marc,' he pleaded, their eyes locked onto each other, 'I have never been unfaithful to Brooke, and you have changed my life. Meeting you, loving you—it's made me realize that I can't deny who I am any longer.'

After hearing Nicholas' heartfelt plea and feeling the intensity of his emotions, Marc felt a mixture of sensations. On the one hand, Nicholas' words expressed a deep commitment to their relationship, and he loved me, he thought to himself. This might have given Marc a sense of hope and reassurance that Nicholas was genuinely willing to make significant changes in his life for the sake of their love.

However, there was a lingering sense of doubt or skepticism. Given the complex nature of their relationship, with Nicholas still married, Marc is still uncertain about how easily Nicholas could extricate himself from that situation. The fear of being led on or hurt still is the ultimate issue. Oh God, what should I do, he asks himself in his head.

In this moment of uncertainty and doubt, Nicholas feels a mix of anxiety, guilt, and desperation. He can sense Marc's internal turmoil and understands the weight of the situation he has placed them both in. Nicholas knows that his commitment to Marc is genuine. Still, he's also aware of the immense challenges and complexities of leaving his marriage.

Nicholas panics in response to the realization that Marc might pull away or doubt their future. He knows that his decisions will have a profound impact on both Marc and Brooke, and he's caught in the middle of a profoundly emotional and morally complex situation.

Nicholas sees Marc's brain working a mile a minute, and he panics as he takes a step closer.

Nicholas' step closer to Marc is an instinctual response to

bridge the emotional distance that's emerged between them. He wants to convey his sincerity and reassure Marc that he wants him.

He takes another step closer, and Marc takes a step back. Nicholas stops dead in his tracks... 'Marc... please.' The tears race down Marc's face. Nicholas takes one final step until they are nearly nose to nose.

Nicholas reaches and takes Marc into his arms and embraces him.

Their faces drew closer, until they were mere inches apart, their foreheads touching in a passionate kiss. Tears and emotions flowed freely as they clung to each other, sharing the depths of their love and the weight of their circumstances. Their kiss embracing each other, as the troubles of the day seem to vanish, all that was present was their lips, their bodies, their hearts.

Their kisses become more passionate as Nicholas back walks Marc to the sofa; he places his arm around his back and lowers him. Nicholas gently hovers over him before laying his weight on top of him and continuing the passionate kiss on him. Nicholas slowly began to kiss Marc's neck and runs his hand under Marc's T-shirt, feeling his smooth, tight chest and abs before slowly sliding his hand into Marc's jeans, feeling his engorged manhood.

Marc shifted under him, a combination of uncertainty and desire crossing his face. Nicholas could feel the tension in Marc's body, and he knew he needed to take things slow. He broke the kiss and leaned back slightly; his hand still wrapped around Marc's throbbing length.

Then Nicholas undoes Marc's jeans to release Marc's engorged member. Nicholas slowly kisses Marc's chest, his nipples, then back to his neck as he slowly tugs at his jeans. Nicholas finally pulls away and pulls off Marc's jeans at his feet and slowly brushes his face over his enlarged cock as he moves back to his hot, warm lips.

'Fuck,' Nicholas muttered, eyeing Marc's bulge with a hungry look in his eyes. 'You're so fucking hard.' Marc bit his lip, a mixture of arousal and hesitation coursing through him. He had never been that turned on before, and the moment's intensity was overwhelming.

In his arousal state, Marc shifts and slowly gets on top and kisses Nicholas' chest as he pulls his T-shirt over his head; Nicholas' beard tickles his face as he kisses him deeply. He kisses down his manicured hairy chest and bites at his jeans. He unbuttons them and pulls his cock free. He slowly takes his enlarged member into his mouth. Nibbling at the head. Marc shifts to pull Nicholas' jeans off; finally, they are both naked, permitting them to explore their bodies without limitations.

Marc stands, his excitement still ever-present, and takes Nicholas by the hand and leads him into the bedroom. They continue testing their sexual limits and explore their bodies as Nicholas shoves Marc onto the bed. Marc reaches around and pulls lube and a condom from the nightstand and hands them to Nicholas.

'Marc.' Nicholas stammered out, his voice trembling with nervousness. 'Are you sure about this?' A smirk played on Marc's lips as he tightened his grip on Nicholas' cock.

'Who needs words when we have this?' he replied huskily, rolling his hips against Marc's. The sensation sent shivers down both their spines as they began to grind together in an erotic dance of pleasure. Their lips met once again, tongues dancing together in a passionate frenzy.

With minimal struggle, Nicholas hovers over Marc, kissing him as he softly and slowly penetrates him, their eyes locked with intense passion as they lock lips with soft, gentle kisses.

After they have both been satisfied, Nicholas hears a faint

voice. 'Yes, Nicholas,' Marc whispered through the passion that still smoldered between them, 'I will wait for you.' Marc was lying there in utter passionate delight.

Their words hung in the air, a silent promise filled with hope and uncertainty. They both knew that the path ahead would be treacherous, fraught with challenges, but they were willing to face whatever lay in store in the name of the love they couldn't deny.

Nicholas and Marc lay together on the sofa, their fingers gently intertwined. The room was filled with a comfortable silence, the tension of their previous conversations now replaced by a sense of serenity.

Nicholas, breaking the silence, looked into Marc's eyes and said, 'I can't believe we're doing this.'

Marc smiled, his thumb tracing circles on Nicholas' hand. 'Believe it. We've taken a step forward, and it's right.'

Nicholas nodded, his gaze shifting to the window where the rain had now stopped, leaving glistening trails on the glass. 'It's just... I never expected my life to take this turn. To have this secret, this hidden part of me.'

Marc squeezed Nicholas' hand reassuringly. 'Sometimes life surprises us, and we find love in unexpected places. What we have is beautiful, even if it's complicated.'

A hint of sadness clouded Nicholas' eyes. 'I wish it didn't have to be so complicated, Marc. I never wanted to hurt Brooke.'

Marc nodded in understanding. 'I know, Nicholas. None of this was planned, and it's painful for everyone involved. But we can't change the past. We can only try to make the best choices moving forward.'

Nicholas let out a deep sigh. 'I just hope I can find a way to make things right with Brooke. She deserves better than this.'

Marc's gaze softened, and he brushed a strand of hair from

Nicholas' forehead. 'You're a good person, and you'll find a way to make amends. I believe in you.'

Nicholas managed a small smile, his heart warming at Marc's unwavering support. 'Thank you for being here for me. I don't know what I would do without you.'

Marc leaned in, pressing a gentle kiss to Nicholas' lips. 'We're in this together, no matter what comes our way.'

As their lips parted, they shared a moment of quiet understanding, knowing that their journey would be challenging but believing in the love that had brought them together. They were ready to face whatever the future held, hand in hand, as they navigated the complexities of their newfound relationship.

Chapter 11

Family Dinner

Nicholas reluctantly parted from Marc's warm embrace, their lips lingering for a moment before they exchanged declarations of love.

'I love you,' Nicholas whispered, his voice filled with a deep affection that only Marc seemed to awaken in him.

'I love you more,' Marc replied, his eyes shining with adoration as he held Nicholas close.

As they shared these tender moments, Nicholas felt a sense of contentment and happiness he hadn't experienced in a long time. His heart was filled with love for Marc, and he cherished the connection they shared. However, reality soon crept back in. Nicholas knew he had to return home to Brooke, and the weight of the impending conversation weighed on him. He reluctantly pulled away from Marc's embrace, their fingers lingering together before finally letting go.

With soft kisses and promises to see each other soon, Nicholas left Marc's apartment and began his short walk back home to Brooke. His steps were slow and heavy, his mind filled with a mixture of happiness and trepidation.

Nicholas had resolved to have the conversation with Brooke about Marc. He couldn't keep his feelings hidden any longer, and he knew that honesty was the only way forward. As he walked, he replayed in his mind how he would approach the subject, how he would explain the two sides of his heart.

During his solitary walk back home, Nicholas' footsteps felt heavier than usual, as if the weight of his emotions had taken physical form. The streets he traversed were a quiet backdrop to the whirlwind of thoughts and feelings swirling within him.

His love for Marc consumed his mind. The way Marc's eyes sparkled when he smiled, the warmth of his touch, and the depth of their connection filled Nicholas with a profound sense of joy and longing. He thought about the passionate moments they had shared, the laughter, and the whispered promises of love. Marc had awakened something within him that he had buried deep for so long—his true self, his authentic desires.

But intertwined with the intoxicating joy of his love for Marc was the heartache that gnawed at him. He couldn't escape the overwhelming guilt and sadness that he knew he would cause Brooke. She was his wife, his partner for years, and he had vowed to be faithful to her. The thought of breaking her heart tore Nicholas apart.

As he walked, he couldn't help but wonder how he had let himself come to this point. The complexities of human emotions and the tangled web of desires and responsibilities were daunting. Nicholas had never intended to hurt Brooke. He had genuinely loved her when they got married, and he still cared for her deeply. Yet, he couldn't ignore the fact that he had fallen in love with Marc.

The tears welled up in Nicholas' eyes as he thought about the impending conversation with Brooke. He could already see the pain in her eyes, the confusion, and the questions that would undoubtedly follow. How would he explain his feelings for Marc? How could he justify the desire to be with someone else? The mere thought of it made his heart ache with guilt.

Nicholas was torn between two worlds, two loves, and two versions of himself. He knew that the path ahead would be painful and complicated, filled with difficult conversations and heart-wrenching decisions. But as he walked on that quiet, lonely street, he couldn't deny the truth of his feelings for Marc. Love had a way of revealing one's most authentic self, even if it meant confronting the painful consequences of that truth.

His steps faltered as he reached the doorstep of his apartment. He took a deep breath, bracing himself for the storm that awaited him inside. The door opened and the slam. They were not alone, there were people here.

Nicholas' heart sank as he walked into the apartment to find it bustling with activity. The loud chatter of voices, the clinking of dishes, and the aroma of a home-cooked meal filled the air. It starkly contrasted the emotional turmoil he was grappling with, and he felt like an outsider in his own home. Brook's parents were there, her mother's sister and her husband were there also.

Sadness weighed heavily on him. The happy family dinner scene before him served as a poignant reminder of the life he had built with Brooke. The laughter and love that once brought him comfort now seemed like a cruel twist of fate. He couldn't help but feel like an imposter, knowing that he was about to shatter the illusion of a perfect life.

His fear wasn't just about the unknown, it was about the profound changes that would inevitably follow. It was about confronting the consequences of his actions and the uncertain path that lay ahead.

Guilt gnawed at his conscience. He couldn't escape the overwhelming sense of wrongdoing that accompanied his love for Marc. He felt guilty for betraying Brooke's trust, for allowing himself to fall in love with someone else, and for the pain he was about to cause her. It was a suffocating guilt that threatened to consume him.

As he closed the door behind him, the weight of his emotions bore down on him. The warmth of the family dinner felt distant and incongruous with the turmoil inside him. Nicholas knew that he was about to disrupt the harmony of their lives, and the knowledge filled him with a deep sense of sorrow.

In that moment, he felt like a man caught between two worlds— one of obligation and commitment, and another of desire and authenticity. The internal struggle was tearing him apart, and he couldn't help but wonder if there was a way to navigate the storm of emotions and find a path to resolution.

'Hey, babe, where you been,' Brooke called out from the kitchen before Nicholas could respond. The doorbell rang loudly, Brooke said, 'Nick, can you get that? It's probably Nathan.'

Nicholas' heart sank as he hurried to the door. Nathan was the last person he wanted to see right now. He knew that Nathan had seen him out with Marc, and he dreaded the thought of what Nathan might say or do in front of Brooke and her family.

He opened the door, and there stood Nathan, wearing a malicious grin. Nicholas felt weak and lightheaded, his plans now thoroughly in disarray.

'Hey, Nick,' Nathan greeted him casually. 'Mind if we chat for a bit?'

Nicholas nodded, his voice tight. 'Yes,' he replied. 'Let's go to the bedroom, here we can talk in private.'

Nicholas said, 'Brooke, I am going to show Nathan my new watch, will be right back.'

Brooke mumbled in the kitchen, 'Watch? What watch? Don't be long everything is almost ready.'

Once they were in the bedroom, Nicholas couldn't contain his anguish any longer. He turned to Nathan, his expression a mix of fear and desperation.

'Why are you here, Nathan?' Nicholas asked, his voice quivering. 'You're never here. What the fuck?'

Nathan's smirk faded, and he looked serious for a moment. 'I need to tell Brooke about something,' he replied cryptically.

Nicholas' heart sank even further. He knew that Nathan's unexpected visit could only mean trouble. He decided to be honest with Nathan, to confide in him and hope that he would give Nicholas a chance to explain to Brooke first.

As Nicholas contemplated this unexpected turn of events, his emotions swirled in a tempest of anxiety and desperation. He knew that he had to talk to Nathan and reveal the truth about his relationship with Marc. But the fear of how Nathan might react, and the consequences that might follow, weighed heavily on his shoulders.

Sadness welled up within him, a profound sorrow that seemed to seep into every fiber of his being. He couldn't help but lament the situation he found himself in. The prospect of betraying Brooke, whom he had cared for deeply and shared so much of his life with, filled him with a profound sense of loss. He mourned the impending end of their marriage and the pain it would undoubtedly bring to both of them.

Fear continued to grip him, intensified now by the presence of Nathan. Nicholas understood the gravity of the situation. Nathan's sudden appearance meant that the truth could be exposed at any moment, and he had little control over the narrative. He was terrified of the repercussions, not just for himself but for everyone involved.

Guilt, that relentless companion, gnawed at him once more. He felt guilty for involving Nathan in this tangled web of secrets, and for putting him in the uncomfortable position of having to choose between Brooke and Marc in this almost hostile manner. The weight of that guilt pressed down on him, making it difficult to breathe.

'Nathan,' he began, his voice shaking with the weight of his confession, 'there's something I need to tell you. Something that's been tearing me apart.'

'Nathan,' his expression a mix of curiosity and concern, nodded for Nicholas to continue.

Taking a moment to collect his thoughts, Nicholas poured out his feelings. 'I have to be honest with you. I've been seeing someone else. His name is Marc, and he means everything to me. I never intended for any of this to happen, but I can't deny what I feel.'

Nathan's brows furrowed, his features hardening as he processed the revelation. 'Nicholas, are you saying you're having an affair with a guy? Are you gay now? What the fuck?' he said in a raised and loud voice.

Nicholas, though regretful and anxious, maintained his composure. 'Nathan, please, lower your voice,' he implored, glancing nervously around to ensure no one overheard their conversation.

Nicholas, in exasperation, tears welling up in his eyes. 'Yes, but it's so much more than that. I love him, a kind of love I never thought I'd experience. I know it's wrong, and I want to make things right, but I need time to do it properly.'

Nathan leaned back, clearly taken aback by the confession. He didn't speak immediately, 'But, what the fuck, man, I don't get it. How long have you been…' He slowed down his speech '…gay, queer, or whatever you are… How could you do this to Brooke?'

'I'm planning to talk to Brooke,' Nicholas said earnestly. 'I need to be honest with her and find a way to deal with things as gently as possible. She deserves the truth, I know that.'

Nathan's expression softened slightly, but he remained cautious. 'Nicholas, this is a lot to take in. I should have known when I saw you a few months ago. I should have fucking known.'

Nicholas nodded, his eyes filled with remorse. 'I am sorry.'

'And you should be,' Nathan's voice raised again.

'I just need you to trust me, Nathan, to allow me to do the

right thing. I don't want to hurt Brooke more than I already have,' Nicholas expressed.

Nathan sighed, running a hand through his hair as he contemplated Nicholas' words. 'I need time to process this, too. Damn it, Nick! Okay, I won't say anything to Brooke until you've talked to her.' He stood upright, with a crossed look, and repeatedly pokes Nicholas in the chest, 'You better handle this soon!'

Nicholas nodded with relief. 'Thank you, Nathan. I know I've made a mess of things, but I will fix it.'

The two men stand there in silence, the weight of the conversation hanging in the air.

'Nick, Nathan, dinner's ready,' a call from the other room.

Nicholas felt a momentary wave of relief wash over him. He knew he still had an uphill battle ahead, but at least he had time to prepare and choose the right words to tell Brooke the most challenging truth of his life.

Nicholas took a deep breath as he followed Nathan out of the bedroom and into the lively kitchen. The smell of food wafted through the air, and the sounds of his family's chatter were both comforting and unsettling. He tried to muster a smile as he took his seat at the table, exchanging pleasantries with everyone. As the meal progressed, Nicholas' anxiety gnawed at him like a persistent ache. He couldn't help but steal glances at Brooke, who sat across from him, unaware of the storm brewing within him. Every glance reminded him of the immense burden he was about to place on her shoulders.

Amid the clinking of cutlery and the animated conversations, Nicholas found himself lost in thought. He knew that he needed to talk to Brooke, to explain the inexplicable, and to reveal the truth about his feelings for Marc. But each time he tried to find the right words, his throat constricted, and the weight of the secret grew heavier.

Nathan, who sat beside him, shot him dagger looks from time to time, silently reminding Nicholas that he had to handle this soon. Yet, the impending conversation with Brooke weighed on him like an insurmountable mountain.

As dessert was served and the conversation continued, Nicholas couldn't shake the feeling that time was slipping away. Soon after, the family left. Nathan gave a final glare, as he mouthed, 'deal with this.'

He knew he had to tell Brooke the truth before the facade of their marriage crumbled completely. His thoughts drifted to Marc, the man he loved, and the tangled web of emotions that had brought them to this point.

Nicholas did his best to maintain a composed facade, but the weight of his secrets bore down on him like an anchor. He met Brooke's concerned gaze, his eyes betraying a flicker of unease. He was painfully aware that his evasive response did little to ease her suspicions.

Brooke's brow wrinkled deeper, her worry intensifying. She knew Nicholas better than anyone else and could sense when something was amiss. 'Nick,' she implored softly, her voice filled with both care and concern, 'you can tell me if something's bothering you. We've always been honest with each other.'

Nicholas forced a faint smile, his mind racing for a plausible explanation. 'It's just work, Brooke. You know how demanding my job can be at times. I didn't want to burden you with it.'

Her eyes softened with understanding, but a shadow of doubt lingered. 'You've been distant for a while now, Nick. More than just tonight. Are you sure there's nothing else?'

Nicholas hesitated, his heart heavy with guilt. He wanted to tell her the truth, to unburden himself and lay bare the complexities of his heart, but fear held him back. He couldn't bear the thought of causing her pain, not yet, not until he was certain of the path he needed to take.

'Brooke, I promise, it's just work stress,' he replied, his voice laced with a determination to protect her from the storm that was brewing within him.

She sighed, a mixture of relief and concern in her eyes. 'Okay, Nick, if you say so. Just remember, I'm here for you, no matter what.'

Nicholas nodded, his gratitude for her understanding conflicting with the guilt of his own secrets. He knew that the longer he kept them hidden, the harder it would become to reveal the truth. But for now, he clung to the fragile peace he had constructed, even as the storm of his own emotions raged on beneath the surface.

Chapter 12

Sam Has Things to Say

The days that followed their afternoon of rekindled love and renewed commitment were a rollercoaster ride for Nicholas and Marc. Emotions ran high, and the burden of their hidden truths weighed on them like an unrelenting storm. In the midst of this turmoil, Nicholas and Marc found solace in each other, their connection deepening as they weathered the storm together. Each day presented its challenges, a blend of guilt, desire, and the harsh consequences of their choices. The prospect of a fresh start, far from the tangled web of deceit, became a guiding light in their hearts.

Nicholas felt the weight of his unspoken truth pressing upon him. The conversation he needed to have with Brooke loomed on the horizon, yet the right moment remained elusive. Fear hung over him like a dark cloud, his apprehension growing daily. He knew he couldn't delay it much longer, especially with Nathan's knowledge of his secret, but finding the right time to reveal the truth was a daunting challenge.

Marc typed out a message to Nicholas:

Marc: *Hey, Nicholas. How about we meet at six in the Village for drinks with Sam? It could be a lovely introduction.* Nicholas' *heart raced with excitement when he saw Marc's message. This was their chance to bring their hidden relationship* *out into the open, to move closer to the future they both longed for.*

He responded, filled with determination and hope for what lay ahead:

Nicholas: *I wouldn't miss it for anything. See you then.* 😊

With a plan in place, the afternoon went by quickly, and Nicholas snuck out of his apartment unnoticed by Brooke. Which was worrisome, but he knows she has a lot going on with work.

Nicholas: *On my way, meet you by your place?*
Marc: *Yes, please!* 😁

Nicholas and Marc found themselves at a designer bar in the Village, waiting for Sam, Marc's best friend, who was blissfully aware of the complex dynamics that had unfolded in their lives. Nicholas was nervous, but as he stood there holding Marc's hand, he was comforted by the intimacy.

Marc squeezed Nicholas' hand and said, 'There he is,' with a big smile and a small giggle.

His warm smile and friendly demeanor immediately put Nicholas at ease when Sam arrived.

'Hey there,' Sam greeted Marc with a big hug and a kiss on his cheek.

'Sam, this is Nicholas; Nicholas, this is Sam,' as Marc presented them to each other.

'It's great to finally meet you in person,' Sam said.

'Likewise,' Nicholas replied with a friendly grin as they shook hands.

Marc nodded in agreement with a smile on his face from ear to ear.

They entered the bar and found a cozy corner booth, soft jazz music played in the background added to the relaxed atmosphere. Before they settled in, Nicholas asked, 'What can I get you both to drink?'

Marc replied, 'I'll have a Cosmopolitan.'

Sam said, 'Just get me a Bud Light.'

'Okay, I'll be back in a minute,' Nicholas said.

The hum of conversation from other patrons filled the air, creating a comfortable backdrop for their meeting.

As Nicholas headed to the bar to order their drinks, Sam turned to Marc, a knowing look in his eyes.

'So, spill the beans, sister,' Sam said with a playful grin. 'What's going on? You've been pretty tight-lipped lately.'

Marc sighed, running a hand through his hair. He knew he could trust Sam, but putting everything into words was still challenging. 'It's... complicated. Nicholas and I are a couple, and I say couple, knowing that I mean a silent throuple, but Sam, I love him.'

Sam raised an eyebrow. 'Wow! You know how to create drama. And I take it he hasn't left her or told her yet?'

Marc nodded. 'Yeah, but it's not that simple. He's trying to figure out the right time to tell Brooke. And honestly, it's been tearing both of us apart, especially since you are the only one of our friends who really knows.'

Sam leaned back in his seat, processing the information. 'I can see why you're all in knots about this. But, man, I hope Nicholas sorts this shit out soon. You deserve to be in a relationship that's out and proud.'

'I appreciate that,' Marc replied, his expression a mix of gratitude and frustration. 'I hope tonight goes well, so maybe we can start moving forward.'

Sam patted Marc on the back reassuringly. 'It will, buddy. We'll get through this somehow.'

As Nicholas returned with their drinks, he could sense a tone in the air but chose not to press for details, hoping that tonight would be fun!

As they sipped their drinks and engaged in light-hearted banter, the tension between Nicholas and Marc dissipated. Sam was genuinely interested in their lives and seemed thrilled to see them together.

During a lull in the conversation, Sam turned to them with a curious glint in his eye. 'You two seem closer than ever. What's been going on in your lives lately?'

Nicholas and Marc exchanged a meaningful look. This was the moment they had been waiting for—an opportunity to share their intentions of building a more long-term, committed relationship. They took a deep breath, and Marc spoke first.

'Sam, Nicholas and I have been working on something important together. We've realized that what we share goes beyond friendship, and we're trying to make our relationship more permanent.'

Sam's eyes lit up with excitement and intrigue. 'That's wonderful! You two are amazing together. But... what about your wife? I'm sorry, I need to ask.'

Marc gave Sam a tort stare with a tilted head and wide eyes. Nicholas shifted in his seat.

The mention of Brooke brought a heavy silence to the table. Nicholas hesitated, his gaze dropping to his drink. 'I... I'm trying to find the right time to talk to her,' he admitted quietly, the weight of his unresolved marriage still looming over him.

Sam sensed the complexity of the situation but chose to be supportive. 'I understand that these things are never easy,' he said empathetically. 'But it's important to be honest with her. And not to dick Marc around.'

Nicholas nodded, his resolve firming. 'You're right, Sam. I must find the right time and the courage to do it.'

In the background, the music grew a little louder, 'Start spreadin' the news, I'm leavin' today, I want to be a part of it, New York, New York.' Marc starts to sing to lighten the mood a little, as the three join in together.

As the evening continued, the conversation took a different turn. Marc says, 'What about you, Sam, what's up?'

Sam revealed that he had been dating a guy named Felipe. Marc screamed, 'Pic, please.' As Marc and Nicholas viewed the pic, they saw Felipe as a striking figure with confidence and warmth. His dark, expressive eyes seemed to hold a world of stories, and his friendly smile was both disarming and inviting.

Marc said, 'You have a Latin lover.'

Sam replied with a little hesitation and redness to his cheeks, 'Yes, he is Brazilian. But I do not know how long because he faces some immigration issues.'

'How can I help?' Nicholas jumped right in.

'No, no, that is not why I brought it up,' Sam expressed.

'Maybe I can help; I have some connections that might be able to assist with the immigration process,' Nicholas says with sincerity.

Sam's eyes widened with gratitude. 'That would mean the world to us, Nicholas. I'll give you my number. Please, see if there's anything you can do.'

Nicholas and Sam exchanged contact information, sealing their newfound friendship with the promise of aid and support.

At that moment, it felt as though their lives were converging, and the possibilities of a brighter future hung in the air.

As the night wore on, Nicholas and Marc shared stories, laughter, and plans for what lay ahead. Their hearts were filled with hope, knowing they were taking the first steps toward a future together, even as they grappled with the tangled web of their past.

And so, in the heart of the Village, under the gentle glow of streetlights and the watchful eye of the city, Nicholas and Marc faced the crossroads of their lives. With Sam by their side, they were poised to navigate the challenges ahead.

Chapter 13

Weekend Get Away

Nicholas had received an email about the consulting project meeting in Boston a few weeks ago. As he glanced at his calendar, he realized that the timing could be perfect for a weekend getaway with Marc. He thought this would be an ideal opportunity for spending some quality time with him. It was time for a break, and he couldn't think of a better way to spend it than exploring a new city, together.

With his phone in hand, Nicholas texted Marc, his fingers dancing over the keys.

Nicholas: *Marc, are you free on Thursday night to Sunday? I need to go to Boston, and I would love for you to go with me.*

Marc stared at his phone for a moment, contemplating the invitation. He had been wrestling with his emotions and the complexities of his relationship with Nicholas, but the idea of a weekend away was tempting. After a brief pause, he replied:

Marc: *Yes, I would love to. Why are you going?*
Nicholas: *I have a meeting on Friday morning, but then I am free. I thought we could explore the city.*
Marc: *Sure, I would love to.*

The week leading up to their trip seemed to drag on forever for Nicholas. The anticipation of spending three full days with Marc made his heart skip a beat. In a city where no one knew them, not having to worry about risk, and the idea of just being alone with him.

The anticipation of spending quality time together built with each passing day as Marc glided around the library. On Thursday afternoon, he made his way to Central Station, where he would meet Nicholas to catch the train to Boston. As he waited on the platform, his heart raced with excitement, but his face housed a smile from ear to ear.

Marc turned, and Nicholas was there, the platform bustling with commuters around them and a gleam of excitement in his eyes. He couldn't help but be swept up in the energy of their upcoming adventure. 'Marc,' he began, his voice tinged with enthusiasm, 'I can't believe we're spending the whole weekend together. It's going to be an amazing weekend.'

Marc's smile widened as he gazed into Nicholas' eyes. 'I know, right? I've been looking forward to this all week. Boston is such an incredible city.'

As they stood waiting on the platform, anticipating their adventure, Nicholas turned to Marc with a gleam of excitement in his eyes.

'You know, I can't believe how much you packed for the weekend,' Nicholas said jokingly.

Marc chuckled, his voice filled with contentment. 'I know, right? But remember darling, I am gay.'

Nicholas couldn't help but admire Marc's suitcase, and matching bag. 'You know, Marc,' he said, grinning playfully, 'I'm sure you have an impressive collection of outfits for every possible occasion.'

Marc chuckled, his voice filled with the confidence of someone who knew their style. 'Well, darling, it's a gay man's prerogative to be fashion-forward. Gotta represent, you know?'

Nicholas laughed, almost falling over, appreciating Marc's candidness and humor. 'Absolutely! And I have to admit, it's one of the things I love about you.'

Their lighthearted banter continued as the train sped toward Boston. It was moments like these that reminded them of the joy they found in each other's company, even as they faced the complexities of their relationship.

Nicholas leaned in closer, lowering his voice as if sharing a secret. 'You know, the idea of just being alone with you in a city where no one knows us is going be kind of liberating. No worries about judgment or expectations, just us.'

Marc smiled, his heart warming at Nicholas' words. 'It will be. We can be more ourselves without any reservations.'

Nicholas squeezed Marc's hand gently, a reassuring gesture. 'True. But maybe this weekend will be a glimpse of what's possible for us. We faced challenges together, and we found joy in simple moments.'

Marc nodded, his gaze locked with Nicholas'. 'You're right,' Marc replied as Nicholas leaned in for a small kiss. Then he leaned in for a second. They sat and talked, holding hands, and every now and then a small kiss over the four-hour trip.

Their train pulled into the station, interrupting their conversation, but the wheels of possibility had already started turning in their minds. As they boarded the train and settled into their seats, they knew that whatever lay ahead, they would face it together, hand in hand, just like they had in the historic streets of Boston.

Once off the train, they hailed a taxi to take them to the

charming hotel Nicholas had booked for their weekend escape. The room was cozy and welcoming, with a view of the city skyline that took their breath away.

Their first night in Boston was nothing short of magical. The charming restaurant they'd chosen was adorned with soft, flickering candlelight that cast an intimate glow upon their faces. The clinking of cutlery and the gentle hum of other diners in the background formed a melodic backdrop to their evening.

Marc and Nicholas shared stories from their pasts, embracing the opportunity to escape the burdens of their current dilemmas. It was a night of nostalgia and laughter, of discovering the intricacies of each other's lives.

As they talked about their childhoods, Marc's affection for his mom, Jane, was palpable. He painted a picture of a strong, loving woman who had shaped his world with her unwavering support and guidance. 'You'd love her, Nicholas,' Marc said, his eyes sparkling. 'She's the kind of person who can make anyone feel at ease, and she knows what needs to happen next.'

Nicholas couldn't help but smile, his admiration for Marc's relationship with his mom shining through. 'I hope I get to meet her someday. She sounds wonderful.'

Marc said, 'She is, and she will like you.'

Nicholas spoke of the idyllic moments of growing up in upstate New York, where sprawling landscapes and close-knit communities had left an indelible mark on him. 'It's a place where nature is your playground,' he mused. 'I have fond memories of building treehouses, hiking in the woods, and just feeling the world come alive around me.'

Marc listened attentively, drawn into Nicholas' world of youthful exploration. 'It sounds similar to where I grew up, but I was not an explorer of nature.'

Nicholas laughed and smiled, reaching for Marc's hand. They just sat there for a while and continued their conversation and held hands.

As the night wore on, their connection deepened. It was a moment of respite from the complexities of their current situation, a reminder that they were two souls brought together by fate.

Nicholas said, 'Shall I get the check? I have an early start tomorrow.'

Marc nodded.

They left the restaurant arm and arm and slowly walked to the hotel. They arrived in the lobby still arm and arm, not having a care in the world. They walked through the lobby, then to the elevator, and went to their room.

Nicholas was the first to undress, entering the bathroom to wash his face and brush his teeth. He returned to the bed, clad only in his boxer briefs, and settled in. Meanwhile, Marc patiently waited, undressing himself and meticulously folding his clothes.

Marc proceeded through his nightly skincare routine before brushing his teeth, and then he joined Nicholas at the bed, similarly dressed in his boxers. Nicholas extended his arms and waved his hands inviting Marc to join him. Marc obliged, lying down atop Nicholas, his head resting gently on Nicholas' chest.

They embraced, holding each other in the quiet intimacy of the moment. Time slipped away as they lay there, cherishing each other's presence. Eventually, Marc succumbed to sleep, and Nicholas, careful not to disturb him, shifted to find a comfortable position. They remained in each other's arms throughout the night, waking the next morning in nearly the same position they had fallen asleep in, their connection as strong as ever.

The weekend in Boston had proven to be an enchanting escape for Nicholas and Marc. As they strolled along the historic Freedom Trail, Marc couldn't help but be fascinated by the tales of the American Revolution.

'I had imagined history could be this intriguing, based on the stories my dad once told,' Marc mused, gazing at the cobblestone streets and historic buildings.

Nicholas smiled, his fingers gently lacing with Marc's. 'It's amazing what you can discover when you're in a good company.'

Their journey led them to Boston Common, where they paused to watch children playing and couples sharing quiet moments. Marc leaned in, his lips brushing Nicholas' ear. 'You know, moments like these make me appreciate life so much more.'

Nicholas turned to Marc, his eyes filled with affection. 'I'm grateful for every moment I get to spend with you.'

Later, at Quincy Market, their senses were tantalized by the aroma of various cuisines, and their laughter echoed as they indulged in local delicacies. Between mouthfuls, Marc looked at Nicholas with a warm grin and mouthed 'I love you.'

Their adventures reached a climax at the Boston Tea Party Ships. Dressed in colonial-era costumes, they playfully reenacted the historic event, tossing fake tea crates into the harbor. Amid the merriment, Marc looked at Nicholas with a gleam in his eye.

'Nicholas, thanks for this. What a great weekend, my colonial lover,' Marc expressed.

Nicholas held Marc's hand as they watched the fake tea crates float away in the harbor's gentle currents. 'Yes, it has. This weekend has been a revelation, and I can't wait for all the adventures we'll share in the future.'

As the weekend came to a close, they found themselves

standing on the cobblestone streets of the city that will be held as their first weekend spot. They held each other close, their hearts full of gratitude for the beautiful memories they had created together.

Their weekend getaway had been a much-needed respite from the complexities of their lives. For a brief moment, they had allowed themselves to be lost in the love they had for each other, cherishing every stolen kiss, every shared laugh, and every meaningful glance.

As they boarded the train back to New York, their hands intertwined, they couldn't help but wonder what the future held. One thing was certain, though: no matter what challenges lay ahead, their love would remain a constant source of strength and solace.

Chapter 14

Crossroads and Crossfire

The apartment was bathed in the soft, golden hues of the evening sun as Brooke sat alone at the dining table. A pile of mail lay scattered before her, but her attention was drawn to a single, ominous piece—a receipt from a florist for a lavish bouquet adorned with a strange message:

'To Marc, let's have a coffee. Tomorrow?'

A frown tugged at the corners of Brooke's lips as she traced her finger along the elegant calligraphy on the receipt. She couldn't help but notice the conspicuous absence of Nicholas in their shared home lately. His late nights at work, the recent trip to Boston, and general aloofness was now more recognizable.

Brooke had been engrossed in her own demanding career, and it wasn't until that moment, as she held the receipt in her hands, that the significance of Nicholas' absence truly hit her. It wasn't just the physical absence; it was the emotional disconnect that had silently crept into their marriage, casting a shadow over the life they had built together.

The apartment, once filled with laughter and shared moments, now seemed strangely hollow. Brooke had been so engrossed in her work, her own world of deadlines and presentations that she hadn't realized how their relationship had slowly drifted apart. She had convinced herself that Nicholas' frequent absence was merely the result of his dedication to his job.

Yet, that bouquet of flowers spoke volumes, whispering secrets of a world she had been oblivious to. A world where Nicholas sought solace and connection elsewhere. As she stared at the receipt, mixed emotions welled within her—confusion, anger, and a creeping sense of dread. 'Marc? Who the hell is Marc?'

What is going on, she thought to herself.

She knew she couldn't ignore the signs any longer, and she picked up her phone with trembling hands. She called Nicholas; no answer. She texted him.

Brooke: *When are you coming home tonight?*

No response! She became even angrier, then she recalls sitting right here, just a few weeks ago, and the tension between Nathan and Nicholas. Did Nathan know something? Is that why they were in the bedroom? *Watch, my ass*, she thought.

As she held the receipt in her trembling hands, a flood of emotions washed over her. Confusion, disbelief, and a growing sense of dread intertwined within her. She thought of her marriage, of the promises they had made, and the life they had built together. How could Nicholas have sent flowers like these to another person? A torrent of questions swirled in her mind, but answers remained elusive.

Unable to bear the weight of her suspicions any longer, Brooke decided to confide in Nathan. She called him, her voice trembling with a mix of fear and frustration. 'Nathan, I found something strange, something that doesn't make sense,' she began, her words coming out in a rush

Brooke went on to explain the discovery of the receipt and her growing unease about Nicholas' recent behavior. 'And then there's your visit the other week. Nicholas seemed so insistent that he needed to talk to you. What do you know that I don't?'

Nathan remained silent on the phone.

Brooke's frustration mounted, and she retorted, 'Nathan, this is my marriage we're talking about. Whatever's happening, it's tearing us apart. I deserve to know the truth.'

Nathan sighed, realizing the gravity of the situation. 'I understand your concern, Brooke. But it's not my place to reveal what Nicholas might be going through. All I can say is that he's dealing with something, and I hope he finds the strength to talk to you soon.'

Brooke felt a mix of anger, sadness, and desperation. She couldn't help but wonder if Nathan was protecting Nicholas or if there was something more he wasn't saying. 'Nathan, please, I need to know the truth. Our marriage is falling apart, and I can't fix it without understanding what's happening.'

Nathan empathized with her pain and inner turmoil. 'I wish I could help you more. But all I can suggest is that you talk to Nicholas. Share your concerns and fears with him. It's the best way, but man, I…' Nathan hesitated, 'Brooke, I'm sorry, but he was supposed to talk to you.'

'So, you do know something, tell me.' Brooke yelled in anger.

With hesitation, Nathan said, 'Yes, there is something, there is someone else.'

Brooke abruptly hangs up the phone.

Their conversation left Brooke with more questions than answers but also steeled her resolve. She knew she couldn't continue in this state of uncertainty and doubt. The fragile foundation of trust in her marriage had been cracked, and if she wanted any chance of saving it, she needed to confront Nicholas and lay bare the truths that had been hidden.

The room seemed to spin around Brooke as the truth settled

in. Her husband, the man she had built her life with, had been unfaithful. The receipt for flowers was a cruel confirmation of the betrayal that had unfolded behind her back.

As she stared at the receipt, she saw the delivery address. She grabbed her phone and looked up the address. It is the library. The library. What the hell she has an internal inquisitive thought to herself. *Who the hell is at the library?* Wait, she thought to herself, *I was there*. She had a lightbulb moment. Anger raged!

With a sense of determination, Brooke left her apartment and headed straight for him. She sees his face ruminating in her mind. Her steps were fueled by anger and a desire for answers. She needed to confront this person, this Marc, who had come between her and her husband. A man she thought she knew. Questions, so many questions.

As she entered the library, her gaze locked onto the familiar face, as Marc stood behind the front desk, his expression a mixture of surprise and apprehension as he noticed Brooke's approach.

Without hesitation, Brooke confronted him in a whirlwind of emotions. 'You,' she hissed, her voice laced with anger. 'You're having an affair with my husband.'

Marc's face paled as he met Brooke's accusing gaze and allegations. He had expected this confrontation at some point, but the reality of it was far more intense than he had imagined. 'Brooke, I—'

But before he could say more, Brooke unleashed a torrent of rage. 'That is Mrs. Jameson, you know that right? You remember me, right? You knew who I was the whole time. Chastising me. How could you do this? How could you come between us? Do you have any idea what you've done?' Brooke shouted.

Her words echoed through the library, drawing the attention

of patrons and staff alike. Marc's shoulders slumped, and he felt the weight of guilt and responsibility for the pain he had caused.

'I never wanted to hurt you,' he began, his voice shaking. 'It's just... things happened and feelings developed. We didn't plan for any of this.'

But Brooke was beyond reason, her anger consuming her. She accused Marc of betraying her marriage, of being a homewrecker, and of shattering her world.

Brooke's voice trembling with anger. 'How could you do this? How could you destroy my marriage?'

Marc's tone filled with regret. 'I never meant for any of this to happen. It just... it happened.'

Brooke's eyes welling up with tears. 'Happened? Do you even realize what you've done? You've shattered my world!'

Marc, struggling to hold back his own emotions, said, 'I know, and I'm so sorry,' he hesitated, 'Brooke, I never wanted to hurt you.'

As the confrontation escalated, Marc tried to explain his side of the story, but his words fell on deaf ears. Brooke's rage was unrelenting, and she couldn't see past the pain and betrayal that had enveloped her.

Brooke's voice vibrating in rage. 'Who the hell are you anyway?'

Marc's voice cracking. 'I never wanted to come between you and Nicholas. It was never our intention.'

Brooke's anger intensifying. 'Our intention? That doesn't change what you've done! You whore!'

In the midst of their heated exchange, Brooke made it clear that she held Marc responsible for seducing her husband. She blamed him for the secrets and lies that had torn her family apart.

Brooke, in her anger said, 'I can't believe that my husband

cheated on me, but then I find out it is with a man. I don't know if it is hurt, betrayal, or disgust. A man. What did you do to him? You tricked him. This isn't him. You stupid little fag.' Brooke stops knowing that she has crossed a line. Her face in shock. She looked at him. 'Just fuck you.' And she turned and stormed out of the library.

As he watched her leave, Marc knew that the consequences of their affair were far-reaching and irreparable. The crossroads they had arrived at would change their lives, leaving behind a trail of heartache and regret.

Marc stood there in shock, confusion, and belittlement. This was once a place of peace, but it was now a battleground of emotions, his heart heavy with guilt and empathy as Brooke's accusations rained down on him. He knew he had played a part in this painful situation, and now, he had to face the consequences. Not knowing what to do, he looked around, hesitates for a moment, and then, in sheer embarrassment, he turned and walked out of the library in utter disgrace.

Chapter 15

Roads of Regret

As Marc stepped out of the library, the cool breeze of the evening hit his face, but it offered no solace for the storm of emotions raging inside him. The world outside felt alien, a stark contrast to his sanctuary or what may now be his former place of solace.

His footsteps echoed on the sidewalk as he wandered aimlessly, the weight of Brooke's words and the reality of his actions haunting him. He knew he couldn't stay here, in the city where every corner held memories of the clandestine meetings with Nicholas. The tangled web of secrets had finally unraveled, leaving chaos in its wake.

Marc wrestled with guilt, realizing that his affair with Nicholas had caused Brooke immense pain. It wasn't just about Nicholas anymore but about the collateral damage their relationship had inflicted on an innocent party. Marc had never intended this to happen, but intentions mattered little now.

His phone buzzed, pulling him out of his turbulent thoughts. It was a message from Nicholas, who had become his lifeline in this storm.

Nicholas: *Are you free tonight? Do you want to meet up?*

Amid his emotional turmoil, his phone had become both a source of solace and a bearer of unsettling news. His hands and mind trembled, and passersby noticed his sorrow. But Marc was so emotionally distant that he only noticed it in passing. He knows he needs to react to Nicholas, but the tears flow so vigorously that he finds texting difficult. His fingers begin to form words on the screen.

Marc: *Brooke just left the library; she figured out everything. You need to deal with her. I cannot handle this situation anymore.*

Tears continued to well in his eyes as he hit send. It was an agonizing decision born out of necessity rather than desire. The idea of leaving Nicholas was excruciating, but staying meant risking more damage to Nicholas' life, something Marc couldn't bear.

Marc: *I am leaving the city; please don't contact me.*

As Marc retreated further into his thoughts, the weight of his decision bore down on him. Nicholas' frantic responses flooded his phone.

Nicholas: *What? What do you mean? Brooke knows about us. How?*

Marc's phone starts to ring, but he refuses the call, then the second, then the third.

Nicholas: *Please, Marc, answer me.*

Not knowing what to do, he turns off his phone in desperation.
As Marc stood amidst the shattered remnants of his life in his apartment, he knew he had to decide. The emotional turmoil,

guilt, and overwhelming despair had become too much to bear. With each item he placed into his suitcase, he felt as though he was leaving behind a piece of himself, a part of the life he had built, and the love he had found in the arms of Nicholas.

The room that had once been a safe place, where their love had blossomed in secret, now felt empty and cold. Every object, every piece of furniture held a memory that threatened to consume him. As he packed his belongings, Marc's anger grew. He was furious at himself for allowing this situation to unfold, for not being strong enough to resist the temptation of love.

Tears blurred his vision as he thought of Nicholas, the man he couldn't bear to hurt yet who had no choice but to leave. Marc knew that staying would only complicate matters further, and he couldn't bear the thought of causing Nicholas more pain.

His phone lay on the table. He reached for it with hesitation. He turned it back on, and the flood of missed calls and texts came flooding in. Amidst his turmoil, Marc's phone continued to buzz with messages and missed calls from Nicholas. Each notification was a painful reminder of the life he was leaving behind. He couldn't bring himself to answer, to hear the desperation in Nicholas' voice, to face the heart-wrenching truth.

With each ignored call and unopened message, Marc couldn't escape the nagging thought that Nicholas might show up at the apartment any moment. The constant buzz of his phone was a reminder of the timeline he was working against. He knew that Nicholas was desperate to find him, to understand why he was leaving so suddenly.

But Marc had made a choice, a difficult one born out of necessity. He couldn't risk staying and causing more turmoil in Nicholas' life. He needed time to reflect, to heal, and to figure out how to navigate the complicated mess they had created.

Still choosing to ignore the messages and texts, he gathered the strength to communicate his intentions with Sam.

Marc: I am going to my parents for a while. Can you check my mail for me?

Sam: Why? What is wrong?

Marc: I just cannot talk about it right now; I will call you when I get to Ohio.

Sam: Marc, I hope you are all right, please be careful, love you!

Marc's suitcase, packed and filled with the weight of his decisions, stood as a silent witness to his farewell to the city that had once held dreams and desires. As he left his apartment behind, each step felt like a solemn march toward an uncertain future.

Exiting his apartment building, he entered the dimly lit parking garage. The echoes of his footsteps reverberated in the quiet space as he placed his bag in the trunk of his car. The engine roared to life, and the car slowly rolled out of its parking space.

As Marc turned the corner and began the journey away from his known life, his heart sank. There, standing in front of his apartment building, was Nicholas. His posture and expression screamed desperation, a raw vulnerability that tugged at Marc's heartstrings.

Anxiety coursed through Marc as he watched the man he loved, Nicholas, standing there, yearning for answers, for resolution. The temptation to stop, to explain, to embrace Nicholas one last time, was overwhelming. But Marc knew that he had made a choice, a painful one, and he needed to stick to it.

With a heavy heart and unspoken words lingering in the air, Marc accelerated, driving a little faster past the man who had been his world, leaving behind a wake of unspoken emotions and the city that had once held their shared secrets.

The journey to his parent's house stretched ahead of him like an endless highway, a ten-hour drive that offered him little distraction from his racing thoughts. As he drove through the changing landscapes, he was immersed in a sea of sadness, tears streaming down his face and insurmountable sorrows.

The road was not just a physical journey but a voyage into the depths of his emotions and decisions. Marc couldn't help but reflect on the choices that had led him to this point, the moments of passion and longing that had intertwined with guilt and regret. The weight of his actions bore down on him with each passing mile, and he knew that the crossroads he had arrived at were irrevocable, leading him toward an uncertain future. As he sat there and drove, he had flashbacks of the incident with Brooke, but the flashbacks of the heartbreak for Nicholas.

Chapter 16

The End or the New Beginning?

Nicholas stood on the doorstep, a palpable sense of sadness and despair enveloping him. His heartache seemed to radiate from his very being as he stood there, facing the closed door that separated him from Marc. He had come here with a heavy heart, hoping for some sort of reconciliation, some way to bridge the chasm created by this situation.

But the silence that greeted him was deafening. He had called Marc repeatedly, and sent heartfelt messages, but there had been no response. It was as if Marc had withdrawn from the world, barricading himself behind that door.

Nicholas felt lost, adrift in a sea of emotions he could hardly comprehend. He had never imagined their relationship would come to this, that the person who had once been his confidant, his love, would now be beyond his reach.

Tears welled up in his eyes as he pressed his hand against the door, as if hoping that the touch could convey the depth of his feelings. 'Marc,' he whispered, his voice trembling with the weight of his emotions. 'Please, I don't know what to do. I need you.'

But there was no response, only the silence that seemed to stretch on forever. Nicholas felt a profound sense of emptiness, as if a part of him had been ripped away. He longed for the warmth of Marc's presence, for the reassurance of his touch, but all he had now was the cold, unyielding door.

With a heavy heart, Nicholas finally turned away from the door, his steps heavy with sorrow. He stepped back from the building, looking up at a darkened window at Marc's apartment, feeling as though he was leaving behind not just an apartment but a piece of himself.

As he stepped out into the city streets, he couldn't help but wonder if this was truly the end of the road for him and Marc. The uncertainty and the pain were almost unbearable, but he knew that he couldn't force his way back into Marc's life. All he could do was hope that, someday, the door between them would open once more.

Nicholas couldn't help but replay the confrontation with Brooke in his mind, the hurt and anger, what did she say to Marc? He knew that he had hurt her deeply, and the guilt weighed on him like a heavy chain.

When he arrived home, he moved through the apartment like a ghost, unable to find solace in the familiar surroundings. Their shared belongings, the photographs of happier times, all seemed like painful reminders of what was lost. Nicholas had never imagined that his life would unravel in such a devastating way, and the reality of it all was almost too much to bear.

With each passing moment, he felt more adrift, more lost in the sea of his own emotions.

The apartment, once a place of warmth and love, had become a cold and desolate place. Nicholas knew that he couldn't stay here, that he had to find a way to navigate the uncertain path that lay ahead. But for now, all he could do was sit in the silence, lost in his thoughts and the wreckage of a life that had crumbled before his eyes.

The dim glow of the living room cast long shadows, mirroring the darkness that had seeped into his heart. He was entangled in a web of emotions, each strand pulling him in a different direction. The revelation of Brooke's discovery left him in a state of uncertainty, torn between conflicting emotions.

As Nicholas sat in solitude, he traced his fingers along the edge of the coffee table, his mind a whirlwind of thoughts. He wasn't sure whether he should be angry at Brooke for uncovering his secret or relieved that the truth was finally out. It was as if he stood at the precipice of a cliff, looking down into the abyss of consequences.

The weight of guilt pressed heavily on his chest. He had never intended for things to unravel in this way, but secrets have a way of finding the light. He knew he couldn't continue living this dual life, deceiving the woman he had committed to while yearning for the love he had found with Marc.

The seconds ticked by, each one a reminder of the ticking time bomb that was his life. Nicholas couldn't escape the reality that he needed to converse with Brooke to lay bare the truths he had hidden for so long. But the fear of her reaction, the dread of causing her pain, and the uncertainty of their future held him back.

The apartment seemed to hold its breath, engulfed in an eerie, almost surreal silence as the familiar click of the front door lock echoed through the room. It was as if the very air had thickened, heavy with the impending storm. With each passing second, the tension grew, and the evening sun, now casting long, ominous shadows across the room, added to the foreboding atmosphere.

In an almost theatrical entrance, Brooke stormed into the apartment, her presence a tidal wave of emotions that crashed over Nicholas. Her eyes, once filled with love and trust, were now blazing with a fiery mix of anger, betrayal, and a profound sense of confusion. This was a battlefront, and Nicholas was about to bear the brunt of her emotional assault.

Nicholas stood rooted to the spot, his heart hammering in his chest, the anticipation of what was to come clawing at him from the inside. As the woman he had shared his life with for years unleashed the torrents of her pent-up feelings, the room seemed to shrink, suffocating him with the intensity of her emotions. Each word that escaped her lips was like a piercing blade, slicing through the air and finding its mark in his heart.

'How could you do this, Nick?' she yelled, her eyes ablaze with a mix of fury and hurt.

'How could you cheat on me? What's wrong with me? How could you do this to me and with a man? What's going on, Nick? I don't get it!'

Nicholas wanted to explain, to make her understand the complexity of his emotions and circumstances that had led them to this point, but his words were feeble in the face of her rage.

He stammered, 'Brooke, please, let me explain.'

But Brooke wasn't ready to listen. She continued her tirade, pacing back and forth like a caged animal.

'Explain? How do you explain this, Nick? How do you explain lying to me?'

'How do you explain lying and betraying our marriage?'

Nicholas' shoulders slumped in defeat, his voice trembling as he tried to find the right words. 'I never wanted to hurt you, Brooke. It's… it's complicated.'

As the anger slowly gave way to tears, Brooke's voice cracked, and her face contorted in pain. 'Complicated? Is that your excuse? You've changed, Nick, and I don't even recognize you anymore.'

Nicholas stood there, his heart aching as he watched

Brooke's tears fall. He felt like an intruder in his own life, like someone who had stolen the familiar world they had built together and replaced it with chaos.

'Brooke,' he whispered, his voice raw with emotion. 'I never meant for any of this to happen. It's not about changing; it's about discovering something about myself that I didn't understand before,' Nicholas tried to explain.

Brooke wiped away her tears, her anger now mixed with a deep sense of sadness. She looked at Nicholas, her eyes searching for answers. 'What do you mean, Nick? What have you discovered?'

Nicholas took a deep breath, trying to find the right words to explain the unexplainable. 'I've discovered that love is not as simple as I once thought. It's not confined to a specific gender or expectation. It's about who you connect with on a deeper level, who makes your heart feel alive.'

Brooke sat down on the edge of the sofa, her eyes locked onto Nicholas, searching for answers in the depths of his troubled gaze. His words hung in the air, leaving a profound sense of confusion in their wake.

'Love isn't confined to a specific gender?' she repeated, her voice trembling with a mix of astonishment and uncertainty. 'Nick, are you saying… you're attracted to men as well?'

Nicholas nodded slowly, the weight of his confession pressing down on him. 'Yes, Brooke. I guess I am. It's something I've struggled to understand for a long time.'

Brooke's mind raced as she tried to process this revelation. Her thoughts were a chaotic swirl of emotions—shock, disbelief, and a nagging sense of betrayal. She had thought she knew her husband so well, but this admission shattered her perception of him.

'So, all those times you were distant, the late nights out... were you with him?' she asked, her voice quivering.

Nicholas closed his eyes briefly, overwhelmed by guilt and regret. 'Yes, Brooke. I was with Marc. It started as a friendship, but it... evolved into something more. I never meant for any of this to happen.'

Tears welled up in Brooke's eyes as the weight of his words sank in. 'How long, Nick? How long has this been going on?'

Nicholas hesitated, knowing that the truth would only cause her more pain. 'For a while,' he admitted, his voice barely above a whisper. 'I can't even pinpoint when it started. It just... happened.'

Brooke yelled, 'How long, Nick? How long?'

Nicholas paused, he swallowed, 'Over six months.'

Brooke's shock was quickly giving way to anger. 'And you didn't think to talk to me about it? To try and work through it together?'

Nicholas opened his eyes, tears glistening. 'I was afraid, Brooke. Afraid of losing you, of hurting you. I didn't know how to explain it because I didn't understand it myself.'

Brooke's expression shifted from anger to confusion, 'Are you saying... you're in love with this man?'

Nicholas nodded, his gaze unwavering. 'Yes, Brooke. I love him, and he loves me. But it doesn't change the fact that I love you, too. It's just... complicated.'

Tears welled up in Brooke's eyes again as she tried to process what Nicholas was saying. 'So, what now? What does this mean for us?'

Nicholas' shoulders slumped as he realized that there were no easy answers. 'I don't know, Brooke. I wish I did. All I know is that I can't deny what I feel for Marc, just as I can't deny what I feel for you. It's tearing me apart.'

Brooke took a tentative step closer to Nicholas, her initial anger slowly giving way to a profound, overwhelming sadness. Her outstretched hand gently made contact with his arm, a touch that conveyed a complex mixture of tenderness and a quiet acceptance of the devastating reality before them.

In this fleeting moment, Nicholas stood as a silent witness to the unraveling of the woman he had once promised to cherish for a lifetime. It was a sight that etched deep lines of regret and guilt on his heart. The fractures in their marriage had grown into unbridgeable chasms, and the stark realization of their separation was becoming painfully clear.

Their conversation had been an excruciating excavation of buried grievances, a process that had laid bare wounds that could not be healed in a single night. As the first feeble rays of dawn filtered through the window, Nicholas and Brooke silently retreated to their separate corners of the apartment, shrouded in the solitude of their thoughts and the uncertain road that lay ahead.

With each step, Brooke's heart grew heavier, her sorrow palpable in the weight of her movements. Nicholas watched her receding figure, his own heartache reflected in her fading presence.

Sleep had eluded them, and their differences remained unresolved. The apartment seemed to echo with the remnants of their broken love as they retreated to different rooms, leaving behind the emotional wreckage of a night that had irrevocably altered the trajectory of their lives. The rift between them had become a chasm, and they were both left to ponder the vast, uncertain void that stretched before them.

Chapter 17

Home

Marc sat in the cozy living room of his childhood home, a room filled with memories and warmth. The antique clock on the wall ticked softly, a soothing background noise. Marc's mother had been bustling around the house, preparing coffee and snacks, a typical gesture of maternal care that brought Marc comfort.

As Jane entered the room with a tray holding mugs of coffee and muffins, she settled into an armchair opposite her son. Her soft, hazel eyes studied Marc's face, searching for any signs of the turmoil that had led him back home. She reached out and placed a gentle hand on his knee, a silent offer of support.

'Sweetheart, I'm glad you're here with us,' Jane began, her voice filled with a mix of motherly concern and love. 'But it pains me to see you so troubled. You've always been my rock, so seeing you like this…'

Marc looked into his mother's eyes, grateful for her understanding and affection. He reached for her hand, giving it a reassuring squeeze. 'I know, Mom, and I'm sorry for worrying you. It's just… everything's been turned upside down.'

Jane nodded, her eyes never leaving her son's. 'You don't have to explain everything right now. Take your time. But know that we're here for you, no matter what.'

Touched by his mother's unwavering support, Marc sighed and decided to share some of the burdens that had been weighing on him. 'It's about that guy Nicholas. You know I was dating him, but I care about him deeply. And... things are complicated, and I don't know where we stand anymore.'

Jane listened attentively, her maternal instincts on high alert. 'Nicholas? Is he the reason for your visit?' She asked in an inquisitive manner.

Marc nodded, his gaze fixed on the coffee cup in his hands. 'Yes. He's... more than just a friend. We've been in a secret relationship.'

'A secret one?' Jane asked almost before he could finish the sentence.

'Yes, well, it was a secret because... because he's married,' Marc tried to explain.

Jane's brow furrowed in concern, and she gently squeezed her son's hand. 'Oh, Marc, I can't even imagine how difficult that must be for you. But secrets have a way of unraveling, sweetheart. Does his husband or wife know?'

Marc's shoulders slumped as the weight of his secret spilled out. 'That's exactly what happened, Mom. Brooke, Nicholas' wife, found out about us. She confronted me at the library, and... it was a mess.'

Jane's eyes widened in surprise, and she clutched her son's hand tighter. 'Goodness, Marc, that's a lot to bear. But I am not placing blame, but you understand that she has a right to be angry. No? What do you plan to do now?'

Tears welled up in Marc's eyes, and he shook his head, the words escaping him with a tremor in his voice. 'I don't know. That's the problem. I left New York, I had to, just to clear my head. But I can't stop thinking about him and what's happening there.'

Jane sighed softly, her heart aching for her son. 'Marc, love is a complicated thing. Sometimes, it leads us down paths we never expected. But you have to consider what's best for you, for your own happiness and well-being, but you don't want to close your heart off to what could have been.'

Marc leaned his head back against the chair, closing his eyes briefly. 'I know, Mom. I just wish it were easier.'

Jane reached out to brush a strand of hair away from his face, her touch filled with tenderness. 'Life rarely is, dear. But you're strong, and you have your family's love and support. We'll get through this one way or another.'

Marc found solace in his mother's wisdom and understanding as the conversation continued. Though the path ahead remained uncertain, he knew that, with his family by his side, he could find the strength to face whatever lay ahead.

During the past few days, Marc had received daily phone calls from Nicholas. Each time, his phone buzzed with Nicholas' name, and each time, he let it ring until it went to voicemail. He couldn't bring himself to face the man who had been his source of comfort and now his turmoil.

Later that day, as Marc sat on the porch, the sun setting in the distance, he texted Nicholas. It was brief and to the point:

Marc: *I'm fine. I'm at my parents' place. I will call when I am ready to talk. I hope you are okay.*

He left it at that, providing no further details, no insight into the whirlwind of emotions and confusion that had taken hold of him.

His heart was heavy with sadness, anger, and a profound sense of loss. The events of the day had left him emotionally drained, and he needed time to make sense of it all. He couldn't deny that he still cared deeply for Nicholas, but the tangled mess their relationship had become was something he couldn't bear any longer.

The decision to leave New York and seek solace at his parents' place had not been an easy one, but it was a necessary step for his own well-being. The weight of guilt and the realization of the pain he had knowingly caused Brooke weighed heavily on him.

Marc couldn't help but wonder about Nicholas' well-being as he hit send on that message. He knew their separation had hit Nicholas hard, but he also understood that they needed space to untangle the complicated web of emotions and secrets that had ensnared them.

Sitting on the porch, he felt a strange mix of relief and sadness. Relief that he had taken a step toward distancing himself from a situation that had grown increasingly untenable, and sadness for the love he had lost and the uncertainty of the future.

The setting sun cast long shadows across the porch, a metaphor for the uncertainty that now shrouded his life. As he watched the day transition into night, Marc knew that he had a difficult journey ahead that would require introspection, healing, and the strength to confront the consequences of his actions.

Buzz...

Nicholas: *Marc, are you okay? Please call me back. I miss you so much. I don't think I can go on without you. Please!*

Marc ignored the message once again, but he knew he needed someone to confide in, someone who could offer a different perspective on the mess he had found himself in. He pulled up a familiar contact, and after a few rings, Sam's voice greeted him on the other end.

'Hey, Marc, how are you? How's everything going in 'Ohio'?' Sam asked with genuine concern, lacing his words, albeit with some hidden sarcasm.

Marc took a deep breath, his voice heavy with the weight of the situation. 'Sam, I don't even know where to start. It's a complete mess. My life is in complete chaos.'

As Marc delved deeper into the details of his tumultuous situation, Sam's silence on the other end of the line became a steady and comforting presence. He let Marc pour out his heart, the words tumbling out like a torrent of emotions that had been pent up for far too long.

'I never meant for any of this to happen,' Marc admitted, his voice laced with regret. 'I never wanted to hurt Brooke. She doesn't deserve any of this.'

Sam's empathetic tone came through the phone. 'I can hear the pain in your voice. None of us ever plans for our lives to take such unexpected turns. Sometimes, love blindsides us, and we find ourselves in situations we never imagined.'

Marc nodded, even though Sam couldn't see the gesture. 'It's just... I've never felt this way about anyone before. Nicholas is like... he's like a part of me, and I can't bear the thought of losing him.'

As Marc continued to share the intricate details of his situation with Sam, his friend listened intently, offering both a sympathetic ear and a voice of reason.

'Marc,' Sam finally interjected gently, 'I want to be here for you, but I also think it's important for you to remember that you knew what you were getting into when you began this relationship with Nicholas. You both made choices along the way, and while I understand that emotions can be overpowering, it's essential to acknowledge what you did. You knowingly had an affair with a married guy. No?'

Marc's voice wavered as he replied, 'I know, Sam. I've been grappling with that guilt every day. I never wanted to hurt anyone, but I couldn't deny what I felt for Nicholas.'

'Yeah, yeah, I get it, but we talked about this months ago, and you were all strong and knowing what you wanted. You cannot destroy three lives. Brooke's, Nicholas', and yours.'

Sam's tone remained compassionate but firm. 'Feelings are never wrong, but actions have consequences. It's time to confront those consequences, not just for Nicholas and Brooke but also for yourself. You have to decide what kind of life you want to lead and what you're willing to do to make amends.'

Marc sighed, realizing the truth in Sam's words. 'You're right. I can't keep running away from this. I need to face it, no matter how difficult it may be, but I need some more time to figure out how. And what should I do... Sam? Sam, my dear friend, what should I do? Please help me make a decision.'

Sam replied immediately, 'No, there is an old expression: you made your bed, now you need to lie in it. That's all the advice I can give.'

Marc sighed, feeling a sense of relief in sharing his burden with a trusted friend. 'I know. I wish I knew what to do; I know I cannot stay here forever, but I'm scared of making the wrong choice.'

Sam's voice was reassuring. 'You don't have to rush into a decision. Take the time you need to sort through your feelings and make decisions that are right for you. But you need to weigh in on the others in the triangle. And remember, I'll be here to support you no matter what.'

Marc felt a surge of gratitude for Sam's resolute support. 'Thank you, my dear friend; what would I have done these past few years without you?'

As Marc's voice filled the evening air, Sam could hear the gratitude and sincerity in his friend's words. 'You don't have to thank me, Marc,' Sam replied warmly. 'We've always been there for each other through all the shit!'

With a sense of renewed resolve, Marc said, 'You're right, Sam. We'll get through this together. I'll keep you posted on what happens next.'

'Please do,' Sam responded. 'And remember, I'm just a phone call away whenever you need to talk or if you decide to come back to New York.'

The call ended with a final exchange of reassuring words, leaving Marc alone on the porch with his thoughts.

But Jane had overheard snippets of Marc's conversation with Sam as she moved about the house, and as he ended the call, she decided to step outside. The porch offered a serene view of the fading twilight, a perfect backdrop for a heart-to-heart conversation.

Marc looked up as he heard the door creak open, and a soft smile crossed his face when he saw his mom approaching.

Jane gave her son an encouraging smile. 'Well, why don't you tell me what that's all about?'

Taking a deep breath, Marc recounted the details of his conversation with Sam. He didn't hold back, sharing the guilt, confusion, and conflicting emotions that had been consuming him.

'Sam made some valid points,' Marc admitted, his voice tinged with a sense of self-realization. 'I can't escape the fact that I played a part in this mess, and I can't keep avoiding the decisions I need to make.'

Jane nodded thoughtfully, her motherly instinct kicking in as she listened to her son's turmoil. 'You're right, sweetheart. Sometimes, facing the truth and taking responsibility for our actions is the first step toward making things right.'

Marc leaned back on the porch swing, his gaze fixed on the horizon. 'I just don't want to hurt anyone, Mom. But I'm afraid that no matter what I do, someone will get hurt.'

Jane squeezed his shoulder reassuringly. 'Life is messy, Marc. Sometimes, despite our best intentions, people do get hurt. What matters is how we handle it and whether we learn from our mistakes.'

Marc turned to look at his mother, his eyes filled with light tears. 'Thanks for understanding. I don't know what I'd do without you.'

Jane smiled warmly. 'You don't have to figure it all out at once, dear. Just take it one step at a time, and remember that I'll always be here to support you, no matter what decisions you make.'

As the night settled in around them, mother and son sat together on the porch swing, finding solace in their bond and the shared understanding that, together, they could navigate the complexities of life and love.

Chapter 18

Nicholas on the Road

Nicholas was drowning in desperation. The days without Marc had been torturous, and he could no longer bear the gaping void that had opened up in his life. He yearned to see Marc, to hold him, and make things right between them. But he was trapped in a never-ending cycle of fear, guilt, and uncertainty.

He and Brooke found themselves still in the apartment, together, but their situation had left them both in a state of shock and uncertainty. The tension in the apartment had become palpable, a heavy cloud that seemed to linger in every room. Nicholas and Brooke had been living in emotional limbo; their once-happy home became a battleground of unspoken resentment and simmering anger.

Unbeknownst to Brooke, her recent confrontation with Marc had acted as the tipping point, driving him away from the city. Nicholas harbored a growing resentment toward her, though she remained oblivious to his mounting anger.

He couldn't shake the bitterness that had taken root within him. He felt a profound sense of betrayal by Brooke and himself for allowing their relationship to reach this breaking point. The love he had once felt had been replaced by a seething resentment, and he found himself recoiling from any interaction with her.

The past few days, neither had courageously addressed the elephant in the room. Brooke was aware of the growing distance between them but remained oblivious to the recent events.

Their communication had dwindled to minor exchanges—a curt 'hello' in the morning, a perfunctory 'goodnight' at bedtime. But beneath the surface, their unspoken words hung heavily, poisoning the atmosphere in the apartment.

Then, the tension reached its breaking point, an argument erupted. Brooke finally lashed out, unable to bear the stifling silence any longer.

'Then just go to him!' she spat out; her voice edged with frustration. 'I know I can't compete with him.' The words hung in the air like a declaration of war, her anger and hurt laid bare.

Nicholas, taken aback by the sudden outburst, clenched his fists to control the anger that surged within him. 'I can't; he left after what you told him, and I don't know where he is. I know he is in Ohio, but I don't know where.'

A bolt of lightning. Sam!

Sam must know where Marc is. He had to try. He reached for his phone, his fingers trembling with anticipation. He pulled up Sam's contact details and hit dial.

The phone rang, and Nicholas' heart raced with each passing second. Finally, Sam picked up, his voice tinged with curiosity. 'Nicholas? What's up?'

Nicholas took a deep breath, trying to compose himself. 'Sam, I need your help. I... I need to find Marc. I know he's with his parents in Ohio, but I don't know where they live. Can you help me, please?'

Sam hesitated momentarily, and Nicholas could sense his reluctance through the phone. 'Nicholas, this is a really bad idea. Marc needs space right now. Pushing him might make things worse.'

Nicholas felt his desperation mounting, and pleaded with

Sam. 'I can't lose him. I love him, and I can't imagine my life without him. Please, I need to at least talk to him. Just give me the address, and I promise I won't do anything crazy.'

Sam sighed, remembering his help with Felipe, the weight of the situation apparent in his voice. 'All right, but promise me you'll be careful. And don't push him too hard. His heart's been through a lot.'

Nicholas felt a rush of appreciation toward Sam as he received the address. He hung up the phone, packed a few things, grabbed his keys, and headed to the living room to leave the apartment.

His resolve to find Marc was unwavering, he knew he needed to have one final, painful conversation with Brooke. Their relationship had been a hotbed of disdain splintering daily, and he couldn't leave without offering her some semblance of closure.

Brooke watched him, her eyes filled with anger, sorrow, and confusion. She had hoped that Nicholas would choose her, that he would fight to save their marriage. Realizing he would let it go for another person was a bitter pill.

'Nicholas,' she began, her voice quivering with emotion. 'You can't just leave like this. We can work through this. We can go to therapy, talk it out, do whatever it takes.'

Nicholas turned to face her, his expression pained but resolute. 'Brooke, I wish it were that simple. But I can't pretend anymore. I can't stay in a marriage where my heart isn't fully present.'

Brooke's eyes welled up with tears as her voice broke. 'You're choosing him over me, over us. After everything we've been through, you're just giving up?'

Nicholas took a step closer to her, his voice gentle but firm.

'I'm not giving up, Brooke. I'm choosing to follow my heart, even if it means facing the pain of letting go.'

Tears streamed down Brooke's face as she struggled to comprehend the depth of the situation. 'Nicholas, please... don't do this. Don't leave me for him.'

Nicholas reached out and touched her cheek, his thumb wiping away a tear. 'I love you, Brooke, and I always will. But I'm in love with Marc. I can't ignore that anymore. It wouldn't be fair to either of us. I am going to find him!'

Brooke's heart shattered at his words, and she collapsed onto the couch, her sobs wrecking her body. Nicholas stood there, his heart heavy with the weight of his decision, knowing that there was no easy way out of this painful situation.

'I'm so sorry,' he whispered, his voice filled with regret and sorrow. 'I never wanted to hurt you like this.'

Their apartment was filled with the sound of Brooke's heart-wrenching sobs as Nicholas turned and walked away, leaving her behind. He knew that the road ahead would be filled with its own challenges, but he couldn't deny the love he felt for Marc, a love that had become too powerful to ignore.

The journey was a blur of endless highways and restless thoughts. Nicholas' mind raced, replaying all the moments he had shared with Marc, the laughter, the passion, and the profound connection that had drawn them together. He couldn't bear the thought of losing it all.

Finally, after driving all night, Nicholas arrived at Marc's childhood home. His heart pounded in his chest as he rang the doorbell, and he was greeted by the sight of Marc standing there, his eyes swollen from tears but still holding a glimmer of love.

Marc's voice trembled as he spoke, a mixture of emotions flooding him. 'Nicholas, what are you doing here?'

Nicholas swallowed hard, his own eyes glistening with unshed tears. 'I had to see you. We need to talk. To talk through this.'

They stood there for a moment, the weight of their unspoken feelings hanging in the air. Nicholas finally took a step closer, his voice filled with sincerity. 'Marc, I know I messed up. I should have been honest with Brooke a long time ago. But I love you, and I want to be with you. I'm willing to leave her, to make things right. Please, come back with me.'

Overhearing this conversation, Jane stepped forward with a warm smile. 'Marc, he must be tired. Invite him in, rest a bit, and have a cup of coffee. Hello, I'm Marc's mom, Jane.'

Nicholas nodded gratefully, appreciating the kindness in her voice. 'Thank you, Jane. I'm Nicholas.'

As they entered the cozy living room, Marc couldn't help but feel a mix of emotions swirling within him. He had been away from Nicholas for what felt like an eternity, and now, here he was, standing in his childhood home, faced with a choice that would shape the rest of his life.

Nicholas and Marc settled on the comfortable couch, cups of steaming coffee in hand. The room was filled with an air of tension, a silent understanding that their conversation held the power to change everything.

Nicholas took a deep breath, his eyes locked with Marc's. 'Marc, I know I messed up. I should have been honest with Brooke a long time ago. But I love you, and I want to be with you. I'm willing to leave her, to make things right. Please, come back with me.'

Overhearing their emotional exchange, Jane couldn't help but interject with a gentle smile and a motherly tone. 'Boys, there is plenty of time to talk. Marc, why don't you show Nicholas to the guest room? He must be exhausted from the journey. Let him get some rest before you dive into any deep conversations.'

Marc looked grateful for his mother's intervention, appreciating her wisdom and understanding. He nodded as Jane gave Nicholas' hand a reassuring squeeze. 'She's right. You must be tired from the long drive. Come with me, and I'll show you to the guest room.'

Nicholas nodded, feeling a mixture of relief and anticipation. He knew there was much to discuss, but for now, he was content to have made it this far, to be under the same roof as Marc. As they walked down the familiar hallway, the weight of the past and the uncertainty of the future hung in the air, but they were determined to face it together.

Marc walked back down the hallway and met his mom in the kitchen. Marc sat at the kitchen table, his fingers tapping nervously on the smooth wooden surface. The aroma of freshly brewed coffee filled the air, but he hardly noticed it. His thoughts were consumed by the presence of Nicholas just down the hall. It was as if the past had collided with the present, leaving him elated and anxious.

Jane bustled around the kitchen, pouring coffee into mugs. She could sense her son's unease, and when she placed a steaming cup in front of him, she reached out to gently squeeze his hand. 'I know this is a lot to take in, sweetheart,' she said softly. 'But remember, I'm here for you, and I wish I had the magic answer for you, but unfortunately, this is a situation you need to resolve yourself sooner than I think you were hoping,' as she leaned into him for a hug, and swerved his shoulder tight.

Marc managed a weak smile, grateful for his mother's constant support. 'Thanks, Mom. I just never expected; well, I never expected to see him here.'

Jane took a seat across from Marc, her expression a mixture of curiosity and empathy. 'Do you want to talk about why you think he is here?'

Marc took a sip of his coffee, the warmth of the liquid comforting against the storm of emotions within him. 'I don't know. I really don't know... This whole situation is such a mess... I don't mean to whine.'

Marc and his mom sat at the table for a few hours before he went to the front porch. The morning was warm, and he swung in the swing, reading one of many books he had gotten through over the course of the past week.

Marc's heart jumped as he looked at Nicholas standing in the doorway. For a moment, he had forgotten that he was actually there.

Nicholas said, 'I'm sorry, I didn't mean to startle you.'

'No, no, it is all right,' Marc replied. He had missed him so much, but the complexity of their situation weighed heavily on him, and seeing him here in his childhood home was just overwhelming.

Overhearing their emotional exchange, Jane yelled from the kitchen, 'Nicholas, would you like a coffee, if so, don't be shy; come and get it.'

Nicholas said, 'Yes, please, thank you, be right there.' He gave Marc a sad smile. Nicholas turned and retreated to the kitchen.

Marc just sat there. 'Breathe,' he said to himself out loud.

In the kitchen, Jane handed Nicholas a warm mug of coffee. 'Cream, sugar?'

'No, thank you, black is fine.'

Nicholas accepted the cup of coffee with a grateful nod, the warmth of the ceramic mug soothing to his trembling hands. The kitchen seemed like a place of calm amidst the emotional storm that had descended upon them.

'Thank you,' he said softly to Jane, appreciating her hospitality.

'You're welcome, dear,' Jane replied, her motherly instincts kicking in as she studied Nicholas' troubled expression. 'Marc told me a little about what's been happening, but I'm sure there's more to the story.'

Nicholas took a careful sip of his coffee, savoring the bitter taste. He knew he had a lot to explain and a lot to atone for. 'Yes, there is. I've made some mistakes, and I hurt both Marc and Brooke in the process.'

Jane regarded him with a mixture of understanding and concern. 'Well, none of us are perfect, Nicholas. We all make mistakes; it's how we learn from them that matters.'

Nicholas nodded, acknowledging the truth in her words. 'I just hope it's not too late to make things right.'

Jane's gaze softened, and she placed a reassuring hand on his shoulder. 'It's never too late to try, dear. But remember, it won't be easy, and it will take time.'

As Marc walked into the kitchen, Jane sensed the need for space and reflection in the air, she decided to tactfully step away, excusing herself to tend to a few household chores. She knew that Marc and Nicholas needed time to collect their thoughts before diving into what would undoubtedly be an emotionally charged conversation.

She left them in the cozy kitchen, where the muted sunlight streamed through the curtains, casting a gentle warmth over the room. It was a peaceful moment amid the chaos of their lives, and Jane hoped it would provide the two men with a chance to gather their thoughts and prepare for the difficult discussions that lay ahead.

Marc and Nicholas sat in silence, the weight of their feelings and the enormity of their decisions hanging between them. It was a rare moment of respite, and they both knew it wouldn't last long. But for now, they could simply be present with each other, taking solace in the fact that they were together, despite the uncertain path that stretched before them.

'How are you?' Nicholas asked softly, his voice filled with a mixture of concern and regret.

Marc sighed, his eyes weary from the emotional turmoil of the past days. 'I'm doing… okay, hanging in there, but—'

Nicholas couldn't let Marc finish that sentence without acknowledging the pain he had caused. He reached out, gently placing a hand on Marc's shoulder, and his voice trembled with the weight of his apology. 'I know, baby. I am so, so sorry.'

Marc turned to look into Nicholas' eyes, and for a moment, the room was filled with the unspoken words that hung between them. There was love, there was hurt, and there was a longing for a way to heal the wounds that had been inflicted.

'I know you are, Nicholas,' Marc replied, his voice softening as he placed his hand over Nicholas'. 'But I am not sure what I am doing yet, I may not ever return to New York.'

Nicholas felt a sharp pang of anxiety as Marc's words sank in. The uncertainty of their situation weighed heavily on him, and he couldn't help but fear the possibility of losing Marc forever.

He swallowed hard, trying to find the right words to express his feelings without overwhelming Marc further. 'I understand. Your well-being is the most important thing to me, and I'll support whatever decision you make. But please know that I love you, and I'll be here for you no matter where life takes you.'

Marc nodded, his eyes reflecting a mixture of gratitude and sorrow. 'Thank you, Nicholas. I need time to think, to sort through everything that's happened. I just hope you can be patient with me.'

Nicholas squeezed Marc's hand gently, offering a reassuring smile. 'Of course. Take all the time you need. I'll be patient, and I'll wait for you.'

As Marc pulled his hand back and sat there in shock, his mind swirled with a tumult of emotions. He looked at Nicholas, his eyes filled with questions and uncertainty.

'Nicholas, I don't know,' he admitted, his voice trembling. 'What about Brooke? What did she say? Do?'

Nicholas sighed, his own heart heavy with the weight of their tangled situation.

'Brooke… She's hurt, Marc. She knows about everything. We had a painful argument, and I told her that I love you.'

Marc's brow furrowed as he tried to process this new information. 'And then what? What did she say?'

Nicholas' gaze dropped, his voice barely above a whisper. 'She told me to go to you, to leave her. She said she couldn't compete with you.' Although, in his mind, this was only a half truth.

A heavy silence settled between them as Marc absorbed the revelation. His heart ached for Brooke, knowing that their relationship had caused her immense pain. But he couldn't ignore the love he felt for Nicholas.

In the quiet moments that followed their intense conversation, Marc found himself reflecting deeply on the choices he had made and the impact they had on everyone involved. He had been caught up in the whirlwind of a new and exhilarating relationship with Nicholas, and the thrill of their connection had blinded him to the consequences of their actions.

As he sat with his thoughts, Marc couldn't help but question whether he had been selfish, or whether he had prioritized his own desires over the well-being of others. The pain in Brooke's eyes, the devastation of their argument, and the hurt Nicholas had experienced weighed heavily on his conscience. He wondered if he could ever find true happiness with Nicholas, knowing the harm they had caused.

But there was another aspect of the situation that gnawed at Marc's thoughts—Nicholas' long-standing silence about their relationship with Brooke. He couldn't shake the feeling that Nicholas should have been more honest, more upfront, instead of allowing the situation to escalate to the breaking point.

With these conflicting thoughts swirling within him, Marc turned to Nicholas, his voice hesitant but filled with a need for clarity. 'Nicholas, I've been doing a lot of thinking. I can't ignore the fact that I played a part in all of this, that I let our relationship develop without considering the consequences for Brooke. And I can't help but wonder why you didn't tell her sooner, why you allowed it to go on for so long.'

Nicholas sighed, his gaze fixed on Marc's searching eyes. 'Marc, I won't deny that I made mistakes too, by not being honest with her. I was scared of hurting her, of losing her. It's not an excuse, but it's the truth.'

Marc nodded slowly, his expression troubled. 'I appreciate your honesty. But it makes me question whether I can truly be happy with you, knowing the pain we've caused. And whether I can trust you, knowing you kept this from her for so long.'

Nicholas reached out, placing a hand on Marc's shoulder. 'I understand your doubts. I do. But I want you to know that I love you, and I'm willing to do whatever it takes to make things right. If that means giving you the time and space you need, I'll do it. If it means working on our relationship and being more honest, I'm committed to that, too.'

'Nicholas, it's not that simple,' he finally said, his voice trembling. 'Our relationship has caused so much pain, not just to Brooke but to me too. I need time to figure things out.'

The tension in the room escalated as Marc grappled with his inner turmoil. He felt the weight of Nicholas' presence, the urgency in his eyes, and the pressing need for resolution. Nicholas had always been more assertive, direct in his approach, but Marc needed time to sort through the chaos of his emotions.

Nicholas leaned in closer, his voice gentle but firm. 'Marc, I understand that this is difficult, but I need to know where we stand. Can you see a future with me? Can you forgive me for not telling Brooke sooner?'

Marc's silence hung in the air, the unspoken words swirling between them. He felt trapped, cornered by the need for a definitive answer when he was still in the process of understanding his own feelings.

'I can't tell you right now,' Marc finally admitted, his voice barely above a whisper. 'I just don't know, Nicholas. I can't make any promises, and I can't give you a clear answer.'

Nicholas' frustration bubbled to the surface, his voice tinged with a hint of exasperation. 'Marc, it's been over a week. We can't keep dancing around this. It's a simple question: Do you want to be with me or not?'

Marc's eyes welled with tears, his emotions a tumultuous whirlwind. 'I wish I had a straightforward answer. I truly do, but I can't give you one right now.'

Their voices rose in a heated exchange, frustration and confusion fueling their argument. Marc's heart ached as he realized the pain he was causing Nicholas, but he couldn't ignore the turmoil within himself.

'Nicholas,' Marc finally said, his voice trembling with emotion, 'I think you should go.'

Nicholas, eyes filled with hurt and disappointment, nodded

slowly. He stood up. 'But you know that I love you,' he said, his voice cracking. 'I know I said I can wait, but I at least need a lifeline that there is a possibility. When you figure things out, you know where to find me.'

Jane, who had been listening to the heated exchange from the adjacent room, stepped into the kitchen with a concerned look on her face. She heard the turmoil between Marc and Nicholas and wanted to offer some comfort.

'Nicholas, I'll fix you a coffee to go,' she said gently, her voice filled with empathy. She knew that the situation was taking a toll on both of them, and a warm cup of coffee might provide some solace during this difficult moment.

Nicholas nodded gratefully, appreciating Jane's gesture of kindness. 'Thank you, Jane. I could use a cup.'

As Jane busied herself in the kitchen, preparing the coffee, Marc sat at the table in a tearful silence, Nicholas went to retrieve his things, Jane met Nicholas at the front door with the coffee.

'Jane, thank you for your kindness,' Nicholas said with a hint of sadness.

'You're welcome, dear, you have a safe drive,' Jane said with kindness.

Marc appeared in the doorway with sadness on his face. 'Goodbye, please know that I do love you.'

Nicholas turned with sadness. 'Bye,' and he mouthed 'I love you.'

Chapter 19

Nicholas Morns

Nicholas had left Ohio with a heavy heart, his spirit crushed by the uncertainty of his future. The ten-hour drive had been a lonely and contemplative journey, each mile feeling like a step further away from the love he desperately wanted to hold onto. As he entered New York, the city's familiar skyline seemed cold and indifferent, a stark contrast to the warmth and intimacy he had shared with Marc.

Upon arriving at his apartment building, Nicholas' steps felt leaden, as if the weight of his sorrow had seeped into his bones. He climbed the stairs to his floor, the hallway echoing with his solitude. His key turned in the lock, and he hesitated for a moment before entering, unsure of what awaited him inside.

When he stepped into the apartment, he was met with an unexpected sight. There stood Brooke, dressed immaculately for work, her hair elegantly styled, and her makeup flawless. She appeared ready to face the day, a stark juxtaposition to Nicholas' disheveled appearance and the emotional turmoil that had consumed him during his absence.

Their eyes met, and Nicholas was struck by the complex emotions that swirled in Brooke's gaze. Surprise, concern, and perhaps a touch of guilt danced in her eyes. His presence in the apartment felt like a sudden intrusion.

'Nicholas,' she said, her voice soft but filled with a mix of emotions. 'You're back.'

Nicholas didn't respond immediately. He felt a wave of conflicting feelings wash over him—anger, sadness, confusion, and a lingering love that had once bound them together. The apartment seemed to hold its breath, as if waiting for the inevitable collision of their emotions.

Finally, he managed to find his voice, although it trembled with the weight of the words he needed to say. 'Yes, Brooke, I'm back.'

As Nicholas stepped further into the apartment, the change in atmosphere was palpable. It was as if the storm that had been brewing between him and Brooke had finally subsided, leaving behind an eerie calmness.

Brooke appeared remarkably composed, her emotions now under control. She had clearly had some time to process the tumultuous events of the past few days, and the anger that had once consumed her had given way to a more measured concern.

'Nicholas,' she said softly, her voice carrying a hint of compassion. 'You look exhausted. What happened? Are you okay? And what about Marc?'

Nicholas, on the other hand, looked utterly spent. The emotional rollercoaster of the past few days had taken a toll on him, and he resembled someone who had been through a grueling battle, both physically and emotionally. He sank into a nearby chair, his eyes heavy with fatigue, and let out a long, weary sigh.

'Oh, Brooke,' he began, his voice trembling with the weight of his words. 'Ohio was… it was something else. Marc and I… it's hard to explain. I left because… he asked me to leave.' His voice cracked as he spoke.

For a moment, there was silence in the room as Brooke absorbed his words. Her expression softened, and it was as if a newfound understanding had blossomed within her.

'Nicholas,' she said, her tone gentle and almost serene, 'we've been through so much turmoil. Maybe it's time we step back and figure out what we truly want. And that may include you, Marc, and me.'

Nicholas looked at Brooke with a mixture of surprise and curiosity. Her words, spoken with a calm and measured tone, were unexpected. They carried a sense of acceptance and an openness to explore a different path, one that he hadn't anticipated.

He nodded slowly, processing her suggestion. 'You mean… taking some time apart to figure things out?'

Brooke offered a small, sad smile. 'Yes, Nicholas. I think we both need some space to reflect on what we truly want. Our relationship has been strained for a while now, and it's clear that we've reached a breaking point. I don't want us to keep hurting each other.'

Nicholas sighed, feeling a mix of emotions. It was a relief to hear Brooke's willingness to consider an alternative to their tumultuous arguments, but it also brought with it a sense of uncertainty. The prospect of a future that didn't involve Marc seemed daunting, but he also recognized the need for clarity and healing.

'I agree,' he said softly. 'We do need time to think about what we want individually. And yes, that may include Marc as well. But Brooke, I want you to know that whatever happens, I care about you, and I want us both to find happiness, even if it's not together.'

Brooke reached out and placed her hand on his, a gesture that conveyed understanding and a hint of gratitude. 'Thank you, Nicholas. I care about you too, and I want the same. Let's take this time to heal and rediscover ourselves. And who knows, maybe we'll find a way to be friends, to support each other as we move forward separately.'

The days that followed Brooke's unexpected suggestion were marked by an unusual calm in their apartment. While the uncertainty of their future still loomed overhead, there was a newfound sense of peace that had settled between them. Nicholas, however, found it increasingly difficult to ignore the weight of his unresolved feelings for Marc.

One morning, as Brooke prepared to leave for work, she noticed Nicholas still in bed. She approached the bedroom door but decided not to disturb him. Perhaps, she thought, he needed this time to rest and collect his thoughts.

Nicholas, on the other hand, had not found the rest he had hoped for. He drifted in and out of sleep, tormented by dreams and nightmares that played out different scenarios of his life with or without Marc, and one without Brooke. The emotional turmoil continued to weigh heavily on his mind.

Nicholas lay in his bed, his mind a battlefield where dreams and nightmares clashed in a relentless struggle. Every time he closed his eyes, his subconscious transported him to different versions of his life, each marked by its own set of joys and heartaches.

In some dreams, he saw himself with Marc, bathed in the warm glow of love and happiness. They strolled through parks hand in hand, shared quiet moments by the fireplace, and whispered sweet promises of a future together. These dreams were bittersweet, as they filled him with longing for a love he feared he might have lost forever.

In others, he lived a life without Marc. Loneliness gnawed at him as he navigated a world devoid of the love that had come to mean so much to him. These nightmares were punctuated by the absence of Marc's smile, his touch, and the warmth of his embrace. Nicholas woke from these dreams with a profound sense of emptiness, dreading the thought of a life without the man he loved.

And then there were the dreams of a life without Brooke. In these scenarios, Nicholas was free to pursue his love for Marc openly and without guilt. Yet, even in these dreams, he grappled with the consequences of his actions, the pain he had caused to the woman he had once vowed to spend his life with. These dreams were filled with remorse and uncertainty, and they served as a reminder of the tangled web of emotions he found himself ensnared in.

As Nicholas drifted in and out of sleep, the emotional turmoil that had plagued him since his return from Ohio continued to weigh heavily on his mind. The dreams and nightmares were a reflection of the conflicting desires and fears that battled within him. He yearned for clarity, for a path forward that would bring him peace, but the future remained shrouded in uncertainty, and the only respite he found was in the waning moments when reality briefly replaced the tumultuous dreamscape of his nights.

Days turned into nights, and Nicholas' routine of restlessness persisted. Brooke, returning home late after work, would quietly check on him before heading to her own room. The unspoken understanding between them allowed Nicholas to have this time to grapple with his emotions and thoughts in solitude.

The next morning, as Brooke was getting ready for work, she couldn't help but notice that Nicholas hadn't emerged from his bedroom. Concerned for him, she approached the bedroom door and gently asked, 'Nicholas, how are you doing today?'

From the depths of his thoughts, Nicholas replied, 'I'm fine. I'll get up today, I promise.'

With that assurance, Brooke left for work, hoping that Nicholas would find the strength to face the day. However, when she returned later that evening, he was still in bed, and the heavy weight of his emotional struggle had not lifted.

Nicholas' battle with his inner turmoil was far from over, and the uncertain path ahead remained clouded by the shadows of his indecision and longing for Marc. Brooke, too, felt the weight of their situation, but for now, she continued to offer her support, allowing Nicholas the space and time he needed to find his way through the complex maze of his emotions. However, she knew that she might need to take more drastic steps.

Chapter 20

Marc Reflects

Marc had spent most of the day cocooned in his bed, his thoughts a tumultuous storm that showed no signs of abating. Jane, his ever-concerned mother, had checked on him several times, her loving inquiries met with short responses and an absent but troubled gaze.

Each time she ventured into his room, Jane could sense the weight of his internal struggle. She knew her son well enough to understand that this was no ordinary bout of introspection. Marc was grappling with the very core of his identity, the values he held dear, and the love he had for someone.

In the evening, Marc finally roused himself from the grip of his bed. His footsteps were heavy as he made his way to the kitchen, where Jane was quietly sipping a cup of coffee. He sank into a chair opposite her, and the two of them shared a long, contemplative silence.

Finally, Marc's voice broke the quietude, his tone heavy with uncertainty. 'Mom, I don't know what to do anymore. I'm lost, confused... and I can't help but feel like I'm being too hard on Nicholas.'

Jane regarded her son with a mixture of empathy and concern. 'Marc, you've been through so much, and I can see the toll, it's taking on you. But it's important to remember that you're allowed to feel conflicted. Love is a complex thing, and it doesn't always fit neatly into the boxes society expects.'

Marc grimaced, 'I know, but I can't shake the feeling that I'm responsible for all of this mess. If I had just been more careful, if I had seen the signs earlier...'

Jane reached across the table and placed a reassuring hand on her son. 'You can't carry the weight of the world on your shoulders. What's done is done, and now it's about finding a way forward.'

Marc sighed, his gaze distant as he considered the path that lay ahead. 'I know I can't stay in Ohio forever. At some point, I'll have to go back to New York. The question is, why? Am I returning for myself, for Nicholas, or for both of us?'

Jane's wise eyes bore into Marc's, and she offered a gentle smile. 'Perhaps the answer isn't so black and white. Maybe it's about finding a way to balance your own happiness with your love for Nicholas, while also coming to terms with what's best for all involved.'

Jane said, 'Perhaps it's a wine evening?

As Marc and his mother settled onto the porch, the soft ambiance of the evening surrounded them. The setting sun cast a warm glow over the quiet neighborhood, and the gentle rustling of leaves in the breeze provided a soothing backdrop to their conversation.

Marc took a sip of the Sauvignon Blanc, its crisp notes offering a momentary respite from the whirlwind of thoughts in his mind. He appreciated the comfort of his mother's presence, knowing that she was one of the few people he could turn to this time of uncertainty.

Jane, ever perceptive, observed her son with a knowing look. 'You've got a lot on your plate, sweetheart,' she said gently. 'But sometimes, a glass of wine and a heart-to-heart can help bring some clarity.'

Marc nodded, though he couldn't help but feel the weight of the decisions ahead. 'Mom, I'm just not sure what to do. I keep going back and forth, weighing the options.'

His mother listened attentively, her wisdom a beacon in the storm of his thoughts. 'You mentioned three options,' she noted. 'Returning to New York for yourself, for Nicholas, or for both of you. Each of them is valid, but you have to consider what would make you happiest in the long run.'

Marc took a deep breath, the scent of the evening air mingling with the aroma of the wine. 'That's the thing. I'm not even sure what would make me happy anymore. I feel like I've lost myself in all of this.'

Jane placed a comforting hand on Marc's arm. 'It's not uncommon to lose sight of yourself in the midst of complicated emotions. But remember, you're allowed to prioritize your own happiness. It's not selfish; it's necessary for you to be you.'

Marc's gaze turned inward as he pondered his mother's words. The path forward was still shrouded in uncertainty, but at least he had taken a step in the right direction—seeking solace and guidance in the presence of someone who knew him best.

After an hour or so of conversation, Jane suggested dinner, and Marc's stomach growled in agreement, a reminder of how long it had been since his last meal.

As Marc stayed on the porch, he contemplated his three options—returning to New York for himself, for Nicholas, or for both of them—he weighed the pros and cons of each path, seeking clarity amidst the tangled emotions and uncertainty that had enveloped his life. He said and rhythmically thought through the different options.

Option 1: Returning to New York for Himself:

Pros: Returning to New York solely for himself would provide an opportunity for self-discovery and personal growth. It could be a chance to reevaluate his life, career, and ambitions without external pressures. Marc would regain his independence, allowing him to make choices based solely on his desires and aspirations. By distancing himself from Nicholas and the complexities of their relationship, Marc might find relief from the emotional turmoil.

Cons: Marc might grapple with feelings of loneliness and emptiness without Nicholas in his life, especially if their connection was a significant source of emotional support. There could be a lingering sense of regret for not trying to salvage what he had with Nicholas, especially if he still loved him deeply. The emotional baggage from his past relationship with Nicholas and the guilt over what happened with Brooke might continue to haunt him.

Option 2: Returning to New York for Nicholas:

Pros: Returning for Nicholas could mean the possibility of rekindling their love and making amends for the past mistakes. Marc and Nicholas shared meaningful memories and experiences, and returning for him might allow them to build on that history. The depth of their emotional connection could be a powerful motivator, especially if Marc believed their love could withstand the challenges.

Cons: The future with Nicholas would still be fraught with uncertainty, as it was unclear if they could repair their relationship and move forward. Reconciling with Nicholas could entail navigating complex emotional issues, including trust, betrayal, and Brooke's feelings. Marc might have to grapple with the pain he caused Brooke, knowing that returning to Nicholas could further exacerbate her suffering.

Option 3: Returning to New York for Both of them:

Pros: Returning with the intention of addressing both Marc and Nicholas' needs could lead to healing and reconciliation. It would demonstrate a commitment to working through their problems together, which could strengthen their bond. By acknowledging his part in the situation, Marc could show his willingness to take responsibility for his actions.

Cons: Repairing their relationship would be a long and complex journey, with no guarantee of success. The emotional toll of trying to rebuild a life with Nicholas while navigating the fallout from his actions with Brooke might be overwhelming. There was a risk that, despite their efforts, the relationship might not recover, leading to further heartbreak for both Marc and Nicholas.

As Marc reflected on these options, he knew that there was no easy choice. Each path had its merits and challenges, and he had to consider not only his own well-being but also the feelings and well-being of both Nicholas and Brooke. The decision would require time, reflection, and, ultimately, the courage to choose a path that aligned with his values and desires, no matter how difficult that choice might be.

He said out loud, 'What the fuck, what the fuck should I do? Ugh!'

Just as Jane yelled, 'Dinner is ready, come and get it.'

Chapter 21

Ex's in Ohio

As the days turned into nearly two weeks in Ohio, Marc found himself caught in a whirlwind of just what the fuck. Each morning, he woke up with the weight of decisions pressing on his chest. One day, he was convinced he should return to New York for himself, to chase his own dreams and find his own path. The next day, he felt a compelling urge to go back for Nicholas, to be with the man he loved and who had become an integral part of his life.

His discussions with his mom, continued to revolve around these conflicting thoughts. Him thinking to himself that one of these days, she will snap just from his constant whining. They'd sit on the porch with a cup of coffee, the breeze carrying whispers of the impending autumn. Jane watched her son, her heart aching for the turmoil he was going through.

'Marc, my love,' she said one morning, her voice gentle, 'I can see how torn you are. But remember, whatever you choose, it should be a decision you can live with, not just for Nicholas or for yourself, but for both of you.'

Marc sighed, running his fingers through his hair. 'I know, Mom. It's just… It's not easy. I love Nicholas, but I can't ignore the hurt I've caused, especially to Brooke. And I don't know if I can forgive myself for keeping it all a secret.'

Jane reached out and placed a comforting hand on his shoulder. 'Life is rarely simple, sweetheart. Sometimes, we make choices that hurt others unintentionally. It's part of being human. What matters is how we move forward, how we try to mend what's been broken.'

Marc nodded, appreciating his mom's wisdom. 'You're right. I just wish there was a clear path to follow.'

She gave him a reassuring smile. 'Sometimes, you have to forge your own path, one step at a time. And whatever choice you make, know that I'll support you, no matter what.'

'How about some breakfast?' Jane asked.

Marc said, 'Yes please. Can you please make some pancakes?'

'Yes, of course, sweetheart,' Jane replied.

As Marc wrestled with his emotions and the choices before him, he found himself consumed by thoughts of Brooke. He couldn't help but wonder what she must be thinking, how she perceived the situation, and how much she must hate them both for the pain they had caused. It weighed heavily on him, the guilt and remorse gnawing at his conscience.

'Ugh!' he muttered to himself as he sat alone on the porch, staring out into the rising sun. The word encapsulated the tangle of emotions he felt. He felt torn between his love for Nicholas.

He thought about Brooke, a woman he had known only briefly in the grand scope of his life, yet one who had been a significant part of it. He had never intended for their relationship to take such a painful turn. He knew she deserved better—deserved honesty and respect.

But there was Nicholas, the love of his life, the one who had opened his heart in ways he had never imagined. The connection they shared was like a force of nature, undeniable and all-consuming.

'Is it possible to love two people at once?' Marc wondered

aloud, though no one was there to hear him. It was a question that had plagued him since that fateful day in the library when everything had unraveled.

He knew there were no easy answers, no quick fixes. The path forward was fraught with uncertainty, but he was determined to find a way to make amends, to heal the wounds he had caused, and to make choices that would ultimately bring peace to his fractured heart.

'Breakfast,' Jane yelled from the kitchen.

'Thank you, Mom. Coming,' Marc yelled back, as he stood to head inside.

As they finished breakfast, they heard a car pull into the driveway. Jane went to look, and she said, 'I have no idea who it is, but the car has New York plates, and a blonde woman is walking up the sidewalk.'

Marc's stomach dropped, 'What the hell, Brooke?' he said out loud.

Standing on the doorstep, to Marc's astonishment, it was her. Her presence was as unexpected as it was unsettling, and he couldn't help but stare in disbelief.

'For the love of all that is holy—how did you find me?' Marc asked without realizing what he had said.

'What are you doing here?' Marc asked, a complex blend of surprise and caution in his voice. 'I left you and Nicholas alone.'

Brooke's eyes reflected the turmoil within her as she met Marc's gaze. She had sought him out, driven by a desperate need to confront the consequences of her actions on both Nicholas and Marc. Her voice wavered as she tried to find the right words.

'I'm sorry, Marc,' she began, her apology heavy with guilt. 'I'm sorry for what I did, for hurting you like that. But this is not all your fault. We are all at fault, and I must take some ownership.'

Marc's emotions swirled, torn between anger and a hesitant

understanding. He stood there in shock, not knowing if he had heard her correctly. 'I'm sorry, what?'

'I'm sorry, Marc,' she began, her apology torn. 'I'm sorry for what I did, for accosting you at the library. But this is not all your fault. We are all at fault, and I must take some ownership.'

Marc's emotions swirled, torn between anger and a hesitant understanding. He stood there in shock, not knowing if he had heard her correctly. 'I'm sorry, what?'

Brooke nodded, her eyes filled with remorse. 'Yes, Marc. I knew there was something, but I chose to ignore it. I thought maybe it would go away.'

A complex swirl of emotions churned within Marc. On one hand, her confession offered a glimmer of relief, as if a burden had been partially lifted. On the other hand, the pain of their shared betrayal still stung.

'But why, Brooke?' Marc finally asked, his voice tinged with frustration. 'Why didn't you say anything, confront Nicholas, or at least move on?'

Brooke's eyes welled up with tears, and she let out a shuddering sigh. 'I was scared. Scared of losing Nick, scared of facing the truth. I didn't want to admit that I was losing the man I loved.'

Marc's heart ached as he looked at her, seeing the vulnerability she had hidden beneath her anger. It was a vulnerability he had failed to recognize before, and it made him question the complexity of their relationship.

'I don't know what to say,' he admitted, his voice filled with uncertainty. 'This is… a lot to take in.'

Brooke reached out tentatively, her hand hovering in the space between them. 'I don't expect you to forgive me. I just needed you to know the truth.'

Brooke took a deep breath, her eyes locked with Marc's as she tried to explain herself.

'I know it sounds strange, but I'm asking for forgiveness for my behavior, for not addressing the issues with Nick, but instead, I took all this out on you. I let my fear and insecurity control me, and it led me going ballistic on you in the library.'

Marc's confusion deepened. 'But if you knew about Nicholas, why didn't you confront him or end your marriage earlier?'

Tears welled up in Brooke's eyes as she finally let down her guard, revealing the pain that had been festering beneath the surface. 'I was clinging to the hope that we could fix things, that our love was strong enough to overcome anything. I didn't want to admit that our marriage was falling apart, that I was losing him.'

Marc felt a mixture of anger and empathy, torn between the pain he had endured and the understanding of Brooke's own suffering. 'So, what now? And again Brooke, why are you here? Where is Nicholas?'

Brooke's gaze dropped to the floor, and she let out a shaky breath. 'That is why I am here.'

Marc feeling sick, 'What the hell is going on, Brooke, I just don't get this?'

Brooke took a deep breath, her gaze softening as she explained Nicholas' despair to Marc. It was a conversation that would be hard on them both, but the gravity of the situation demanded transparency.

'Marc, I need you to understand just how deeply this has affected Nicholas,' she started, her voice filled with concern. 'When he left you here, it hit him hard. He felt like he had lost a part of himself, a part of our life together. But it's more than just missing you. It's the guilt, the confusion, and the fear of losing everything he holds dear.'

Marc listened attentively, his eyes locked onto Brooke's. He had never seen her so vulnerable, so open about the turmoil they had all been through.

'He hasn't been sleeping well,' Brooke continued, her voice trembling slightly. 'He spends most of his days in bed, and when he's not sleeping, he's lost in his thoughts. He won't talk to me about what's going on in his head, and it terrifies me.'

Marc's heart sank as he heard the pain in Brooke's voice. He had never wanted to hurt Nicholas or anyone else like this.

'He's withdrawn,' Brooke added, her eyes welling up with tears. 'He used to be so full of life, so enthusiastic about everything. Now, it's like he's just going through the motions. I'm scared for him, for all of us.'

Silence hung in the air as Marc absorbed Brooke's words. He had known that his departure would cause pain, but the extent of Nicholas' suffering was beyond what he had ever anticipated. Guilt clawed at him, and he couldn't help but feel responsible for the darkness that had consumed Nicholas.

'I'm so sorry, Brooke,' Marc finally whispered, his voice choked with emotion. 'I had no idea it would be this bad. I never wanted to hurt him like this.'

Tears welled up in Brooke's eyes as she reached out and placed a hand on Marc's shoulder. 'I know you didn't. None of us wanted any of this. But right now, Nicholas needs you more than ever. Please, just consider going back and talking to him. Maybe you can help him find his way back to the light.'

Marc nodded, his heart heavy with the weight of the situation. He knew he needed time to think, to sort through his own feelings and uncertainties. But one thing was clear—Nicholas was suffering, and he couldn't ignore that.

Brooke's words hung heavily in the air, casting a shadow over Marc as he grappled with the revelation. Nicholas, the man he had once shared laughter and love with, was now drowning in despair. Marc's heart ached at the mere thought of his once-vibrant lover reduced to this broken state. Guilt gnawed at him; he had known he caused pain, but the depth of Nicholas' suffering was beyond what he had ever imagined.

Running a hand through his hair, Marc's face contorted with internal conflict. 'I had no idea he was taking it this hard,' he confessed, his voice laced with remorse. 'But Brooke, you have to understand, it's not just about me. It's about us, about what we've done.'

Brooke's intense gaze bore into him, a plea for empathy and compassion. 'I do understand. It's an intricate mess, but seeing Nicholas like this shatters my heart. We can sort out the complexities later; right now, he needs you. He needs to feel that you still care.'

Emotions churned within Marc as he weighed his choices. Could he truly return to the life he had left behind in New York, attempting to rebuild something with Nicholas?

Could he summon the strength to put aside the pain, the betrayal, and the guilt for the sake of the man he had once cherished?

'I need time to think,' Marc finally admitted, his voice laden with indecision. 'I can't make this decision right now. But thank you for your honesty.'

Brooke nodded, a mixture of relief and apprehension in her eyes.

Jane overheard the conversation. 'Hello, dear, I'm Jane, Marc's mom. Would you like to come into the kitchen and have coffee?'

Brooke looked up and said, 'Yes, I would love a cup.' She stood and followed Jane into the kitchen.

Jane led Brooke into the sunlit room, where the smell of freshly brewed coffee filled the air. The room had a warmth to it, both in decor and atmosphere, a stark contrast to the heaviness of the conversation she had just overheard.

As Jane prepared a cup of coffee for Brooke, she couldn't help but feel a pang of sympathy for the young woman. Brooke seemed caught in the crossfire of a complex and emotionally charged situation.

Jane handed a steaming cup of coffee to Brooke and gestured for her to take a seat at the small kitchen table. She pulled out a chair for herself and sat down across from Brooke, her expression kind and understanding.

'Thank you for joining me, Brooke,' Jane said softly, her eyes filled with compassion. 'I can't imagine how difficult this must be for you, caught in the middle of all this.'

Brooke sighed, her shoulders slumping with the weight of the situation. She took a sip of her coffee before responding. 'It's... it's been incredibly hard. I never expected any of this to happen.'

Jane nodded sympathetically. 'Life has a way of throwing us into unexpected situations. I can see that you care deeply for Nicholas, and you've been through a lot together.'

Brooke's eyes welled up with tears, and she nodded, her voice trembling slightly. 'I do love him. But I can't bear to see him like this, so lost and broken.'

Jane reached out and gently placed a hand on Brooke's, offering her comfort. 'I can tell you care for Marc as well. This is a complicated situation, and I won't pretend to have all the answers. But I believe that love has a way of guiding us, even in the most challenging times.'

Brooke sniffled and wiped away a tear. 'I just want both of them to find happiness, even if it's not with me.'

Jane gave her a warm smile. 'Sometimes, finding happiness

means taking different paths. Whatever happens, just remember that you deserve happiness too.'

As Marc sat in the sunny living room, the weight of the world pressing down on his shoulders, he knew he couldn't stay in this state of indecision forever. The turmoil in his heart had reached a breaking point, and he needed to find some clarity amidst the chaos.

'What am I going to do? What am I supposed to do?' he mumbled to himself, his voice barely above a whisper.

The room felt stifling, and Marc rose from the couch, pacing back and forth as if movement could somehow help him make sense of the chaos that had unfolded. He couldn't deny the anguish he felt for Nicholas, the pain he had caused, and now the unexpected plea from Brooke.

With each step, he replayed the events of the past weeks in his mind, from the library confrontation to his decision to leave New York, and finally, the emotional conversation with Brooke. He had thought he was making a clean break, escaping the tangled web in his head, but now it seemed like the threads were pulling him back in.

His heart ached for Nicholas, imagining him in a state of despair. But he also couldn't ignore the guilt that consumed him, the knowledge that he had betrayed Brooke in the worst way possible.

Marc sank back onto the couch, running his fingers through his hair in frustration. He felt like he was standing at a crossroads, torn between his love for Nicholas and the changing compassion for Brooke. The path forward was shrouded in uncertainty, and he didn't know which way to turn.

A glimmer of hope surfaced in his mind as he remembered the moments of love and happiness he had shared with Nicholas.

But it was quickly overshadowed by the fear of more heartache, and the complications and consequences that lay ahead.

'I love him,' Marc whispered to himself, the truth resonating deep within his soul. 'I need to go home to New York.'

With that realization, Marc knew that he couldn't remain in this state of numbness any longer. It was time to face the difficult decisions that lay ahead, to confront the mess he had made, and to find a way to heal the hearts he had touched. He yelled to the kitchen, 'Okay, I need to do this, I'll go see Nicholas.'

Chapter 22

New York, New York.

Marc climbed into his car, hands gripping the steering wheel as he prepared to embark on this daunting journey. The engine roared to life, and he cast one last look at his mother, who stood on the porch with a mix of worry and hope in her eyes.

Jane called out to him, her voice carrying the warmth of a mother's love. 'Marc, my dear, remember that you're stronger than you think. Take your time and follow your heart. It knows the way.'

Marc offered a weak but appreciative smile, her words serving as a reassuring anchor in the sea of uncertainty that lay ahead. 'Thanks, Mom. I'll do my best. I love you.'

With those parting words, he pulled out of the driveway and onto the open road, the weight of his choices and the longing in his heart propelling him forward, back to the city that held both his past mistakes and the possibility of a future he so desperately craved.

The road stretched out before him, an endless ribbon of asphalt leading him back to a life he had left behind, back to a city filled with memories, both sweet and bitter. The miles seemed to pass in a blur as his thoughts churned with the complexities of the journey ahead.

His fingers gripped the steering wheel, knuckles white with tension, as he navigated the highways and byways that would take him back to the heart of the city. The landscape shifted from the rolling hills of Ohio to the mountains of Pennsylvania.

Marc's mind raced with questions, doubts, and fears. Could he really go back and face Nicholas? Could he find a way to make amends, to rebuild the shattered pieces of their relationship? And what about Brooke, the woman he had betrayed, the woman who had come to him with a plea he couldn't ignore?

The hours on the road ticked by, the monotony of the drive allowing his thoughts to wander and collide like bumper cars in his mind. He replayed conversations, imagined scenarios, and tried to picture the path forward.

As the city skyline came into view, Marc's heart quickened with a mixture of anticipation and trepidation. The familiar sights and sounds of New York welcomed him back, but he knew that the challenges that awaited him were anything but familiar.

The drive had been long and torturous, but it was only the beginning of the journey. Marc had come to a decision, a resolution to confront the mess he had made, to face the people he had hurt, and to find a way to make things right.

As Marc parked his car in the familiar garage and gathered his belongings, a sense of déjà vu washed over him. He couldn't help but feel that he had come full circle, returning to the place where everything had started to unravel. The weight of his decisions bore down on him as he made his way up to his apartment.

Unlocking the door, he stepped inside, greeted by the heavy silence that hung in the air. The apartment felt strangely familiar and foreign; he had once felt at home, but now it felt more like a place of uncertainty.

Marc couldn't ignore the memories that flooded back—the laughter, the shared meals, the quiet moments with Nicholas. But alongside those memories were the shadows of pain and betrayal that had torn them apart.

He sighed as he set his belongings down, unsure of what awaited him in this space. Marc knew he couldn't avoid the inevitable, the conversation that needed to happen, the decisions that needed to be made. With a heavy heart, he picked up his phone and dialed Nicholas' number, hoping for a chance to find some clarity amidst of the chaos.

As Marc settled in for the evening, he texted Sam:

Marc: Hey, I am back in NYC!

A short while later, Marc's phone buzzed with a response from Sam.

Sam: *Welcome back! How was Ohio?*
Marc: *It was... insane, and I don't even know where to begin.*
Marc: *Sam, you won't believe this, but Brooke just showed up at my mom's place. It's getting even more complicated.*
Marc: *She came... wait for it... in peace.*
Sam: *Whoa, really? What did she want?*
Marc: *She came to talk to me about Nicholas. She says he was in a terrible state and wanted me to return to New York.*
Sam: *That's a lot to take in. What was she thinking? Did you call the cops?*
Marc: *She's worried about Nicholas. She thinks it's the best thing for him.*
Sam: *Wow, that's a twist. And how are you feeling about it?*
Marc: *Conflicted, to be honest. I can't ignore Nicholas' suffering, but it's not just about him. There's so much to consider.*

Sam: *I can imagine. Take your time to weigh everything. You've got a tough decision ahead.*

Marc: *Thanks, Sam. I appreciate your support. I'm not sure what I'll do yet, but I'll figure it out.*

Sam: *I have no doubt you will. You've got a good heart, Marc.*

Marc: *Good night my friend!*

Restless and haunted by the turmoil of his emotions, Marc eventually went to bed. The weight of his decision, his love for Nicholas, and the complex situation had taken a toll on his mind. As he drifted into slumber, his dreams were filled with vivid, unsettling images of Nicholas, lost and in pain. Marc tossed and turned throughout the night, unable to find solace even in sleep, his heart heavy with uncertainty about the path ahead.

The next morning, Marc rose from bed, still carrying the weight of his restless night. He made himself a strong cup of coffee, hoping it would bring some clarity to his thoughts. As he sipped the hot brew, he picked up his phone and composed a text to Brooke:

Marc: Hi Brooke, it's Marc. I've been thinking about what you said yesterday. I want to visit Nicholas. Can we plan a time for me to see him?

Marc hits send, his fingers trembling slightly as he waited for Brooke's response. The uncertainty of the situation loomed over him, but he knew that facing Nicholas was a step he needed to take.

Marc's heart skipped a beat as Brooke's response came in almost instantly:

Brooke: Yes, Okay, how about Eleven?

She seemed as eager as he was to facilitate this meeting. He quickly typed his reply:

Marc: Eleven works. I'll be there. Thanks, Brooke.

Brooke: Nicholas is up having coffee and a little better this morning. I have not told him that you're coming.

With a mix of anticipation and apprehension, Marc set his phone down and finished his coffee. The minutes seemed to stretch as he counted down the time until he would see Nicholas again. As Marc made his way toward Nicholas and Brooke's apartment, a swirl of conflicting emotions danced within him. It was a strange feeling; one he couldn't quite put into words. The memories of his life in New York, the love he had shared with Nicholas, and the pain he had caused all seemed to converge into a maelstrom of missed emotions.

Fear tugged at the edges of his consciousness. Fear of what he might find when he saw Nicholas again. Fear of the uncertainty that lay ahead. But underneath it all, there was love. A deep, abiding love that had never truly faded.

Marc couldn't deny that he still cared for Nicholas. He had seen the depths of Nicholas' despair, and it had torn at his heart. He couldn't stand the thought of someone he had loved so deeply suffering in such a way.

As he approached their apartment, Marc took a deep breath and squared his shoulders. Whatever lay ahead, he was determined to face it. He was driven by guilt, responsibility, and a lingering affection for the man who had once meant the world to him.

With each step, he drew closer to the moment of truth, unsure of what awaited him on the other side of that door but resolute in his decision to confront it head-on.

Fear was ever present as he approached the building, but he stepped up to the entrance door and pressed the buzzer.

In the apartment, the door buzzed, and Nicholas jumped. 'Brooke, are you expecting someone?'

As Brooke walked to the door, she said, 'Yes, I am.' She buzzed the door, opened the hallway door, and stood there momentarily.

Nicholas heard Brooke say, 'Hello, how are you? How was the trip? As she hugs the person in the doorway.'

He thought to himself, *Did she call my mother?* Then he looked up and saw Marc standing in the doorway. His thoughts froze. He shook his head to make sure he was not dreaming.

'Marc! You're here!'

Chapter 23

Can Love Be Rebuilt?

'Marc, it's… it's you,' Nicholas stammered, his voice a mix of surprise and confusion. 'I can't believe you're here. What happened? Is this about Brooke? I'm so confused right now. Can someone please explain?'

Marc's eyes bore into Nicholas', a tumultuous sea of emotions within them. He took a deep breath, trying to find the right words. 'Nicholas, I came back because of Brooke. She came to Ohio to talk to me, to tell me about your situation and how much you're hurting. I… I had to see you.'

Nicholas' gaze softened as he processed Marc's words. 'Brooke did this? She came all the way to Ohio for me?'

Marc nodded, his heart heavy with the weight of the situation. 'Yes, she did. She's worried about you, Nicholas, and she loves you.'

Nicholas let out a sigh, his mind racing to make sense of it all. 'Why? Why did you do that?' Nicholas tried to process.

Marc gave a hesitant glare!

'No, wait, that is not what I mean; I mean, I didn't know that where you were.' Nicholas tried to clarify. 'But I am glad you are here, Marc. Thank you, Brooke, but, but why?' he again tried to process.

As they stood there, facing each other, the room seemed to hold its breath, the tension between them palpable. The question of whether love could be rebuilt hung in the air, waiting for an answer.

Brooke took a deep breath, her eyes filled with a mixture of anxiety and determination. 'I know I overstepped, but I was worried about you. You've been in such a terrible state since Marc left, and I couldn't bear to see you like this.'

Nicholas ran a hand through his hair, his exhaustion evident. 'You should have talked to me first. Because I don't think Marc wants to be here, and I don't want him here out of pity.'

'I know,' Brooke admitted, her voice softening. 'I should have, and I'm sorry. But I couldn't stand by and watch you suffer like this. I had to do something. The good news is Marc is here, and I will get out of here and let the two of you talk.'

Brooke grabs her bag, gives Nick a kiss on his forehead, and hugs Marc. 'Thank you, good luck.'

'Marc,' Nicholas breathed, his voice barely a whisper.

'Nicholas, before we even talk, you need to go, have a shower, and get dressed,' Marc explained.

'A shower? Marc, we have so much to discuss,' Nicholas said.

'I know, but trust me on this. It will help clear your mind, and we both need a fresh start. Shower now,' Marc ordered.

Nicholas reluctant but understanding. 'All right, Marc. I'll take a quick shower.'

Marc follows Nicholas to the bedroom. Marc lays out some fresh clothes in the bedroom as Nicholas gets undressed. Marc goes into the bathroom and turns on the shower. When he turns, he sees the image of Nicholas' naked body standing in the doorway; even in his exhausted state, Marc couldn't help but notice the definition of Nicholas' body. He had firm muscles, neatly trimmed body hair, and a stellar manhood. Marc couldn't help but feel a shiver of anticipation. The physical closeness reignited memories of their intimacy.

Marc said, 'Come on, don't just stand there, jump in, wash off that muck.'

Nicholas gave a small grin and did as he was told. Marc waited outside the bathroom. 'I'll be right out here when you're done,' Marc explained.

Marc could hear the shower sound as he sat on the end of the bed and couldn't help but feel a mix of emotions. He was glad Nicholas was taking his suggestion and having a shower to freshen up, but he was also anxious about the impending conversation. Marc's mind was racing with questions and doubts, wondering how this meeting would unfold and if there was still a chance to rebuild, what had been broken between them.

As Nicholas stood under the warm spray of the shower, he couldn't help but feel a whirlwind of emotions and thoughts swirling in his mind. He was bewildered by the sudden turn of events from Brooke's unexpected visit to Ohio and Marc's return to New York.

Amid the cascading water, Nicholas tried to organize his jumbled thoughts. He wondered about the purpose of Marc's return and what it meant for their relationship. He questioned whether Marc still loved him or if this was merely a gesture of concern for his well-being.

Nicholas knew that today's reunion was a critical chance to address the complex web of lies and love that had entangled them all. He was conflicted between the love he still felt for Marc and his guilt for the pain he had caused. As he continued to shower, he hoped that the waters washing over him would somehow cleanse their troubled past and pave the way for a clearer, brighter future.

After a few minutes, Nicholas emerged from the bathroom, a towel wrapped around his waist. His hair was wet, and his face looked a bit more refreshed.

Nicholas smiled, feeling more composed, and said, 'Okay, I'm done, what now?'

Marc smiled softly. 'Although the view is nice, maybe getting dressed?'

Nicholas smiled and laughed as he dropped his towel and threw it on the bathroom floor. He walked toward the bed to pick up the clothes that Marc had laid out for him. He pulled on his boxers, sweatpants, and hoodie. He ran his fingers through his hair to brush it off his face.

Marc watched in contentment. 'Now we sit down and talk. There's a lot we need to say to each other'.

Nicholas nodded as he finished dressing, his heart heavy with anticipation. He knew that this conversation was long overdue, and there were so many emotions he needed to express and understand. As he walked back toward the bed, he couldn't help but notice Marc's calm demeanor, and it gave him a glimmer of hope.

Sitting down on the edge of the bed, Nicholas looked at Marc, his eyes searching for answers. 'I'm ready to talk, but I need to understand why you're here. What made you decide to come back to New York?'

Marc sighed, running a hand through his hair as he prepared to express his feelings and thoughts. 'Nicholas, it's complicated. I needed time to think and sort through my baggage and the mess we've made of our lives. But when Brooke came to see me and told me you were in a bad place... I couldn't stay away any longer. I had to see for myself and figure out what to do.'

Nicholas' gaze softened, and he reached out to place a

reassuring hand on Marc's. 'I appreciate you coming back. I've missed you so much, and I'm still in love with you. But we must face the truth and the pain we've caused, sorry, that I've caused. Can we find a way to move forward, or is it too late?'

Nicholas listened intently, his eyes locked onto Marc's as he spoke. 'I know that I have behaved like a child... impulsively, recklessly. I didn't consider the consequences of my actions, the pain I would cause you, Brooke, and even myself.'

Marc's voice was laced with regret as he continued, 'But, Nicholas, my feelings for you... they've never really changed. I've tried to deny and run away from them, but they've always been there, deep inside.'

Nicholas felt a surge of emotions welling up within him. He knew Marc had made mistakes, but hearing him confess his ongoing feelings was both heartbreaking and daunting. 'Marc, I can't deny that I still love you too. I never stopped.'

Marc reached for Nicholas' hand, their fingers intertwining. 'I don't know if we can go back to how things were. I don't even know if that's what we should do. But I do know that I want to try and make amends, to find a way to heal and find happiness.'

Nicholas nodded slowly, a glimmer of hope returning to his eyes. 'I want that too, Marc. But, it won't be easy. We've hurt each other deeply, and we've hurt Brooke as well. We need to be honest with ourselves and her about what we want.'

'But,' Marc said, 'what about this sudden change of heart from Brooke? Do you think it is genuine?'

Nicholas leaned back on the bed, a furrow forming on his brow as he contemplated Marc's question. It was a valid concern, one that had been nagging at him.

'I honestly don't know, Marc,' Nicholas admitted, his voice tinged with uncertainty. 'It's... surprising, to say the least. I never expected her to go there, let alone extend an olive branch. But people can change, and maybe she's had some time to reflect on everything. I just don't want to get my hopes up too high.'

Marc nodded in understanding, his gaze fixed on the floor as he processed Nicholas' words. 'I get that, Nicholas. I'm just worried about all of this. It's like we're walking on a tightrope, and one wrong step could send everything crashing down, but she has been very nice since Ohio.'

The path ahead became even more uncertain. Nicholas and Marc had just started to tentatively rebuild their connection, their feelings rekindling like a slow-burning fire. Now, Brooke's willingness to forgive and her plea for them to come together added another layer of complexity to their already intricate situation.

Nicholas couldn't help but feel a mixture of relief and apprehension. He had been struggling with his emotions, torn between his love for Marc and his guilt over what they had done to Brooke. He had expected anger, resentment, or even hatred from her, not this unexpected olive branch. It left him questioning her motives and whether he could truly trust this sudden change.

Marc, too, was grappling with his own feelings. He had returned to New York with a sense of determination to confront the mess they had created and seek a way to rebuild. But now, Brooke's involvement had cast doubt over everything. He wondered if her intentions were genuine or if she had her own agenda.

The two of them sat on the edge of the bed, silent for a moment as they processed the whirlwind of emotions and questions racing through their minds. The future was still uncertain, but one thing was clear: they needed an open and honest conversation with Brooke to understand her perspective and decide how to move forward.

Nicholas took a deep breath, breaking the silence that hung

between them. 'Marc, we can't just let this pass without addressing it. We have to talk, not just about Brooke but about us, too.'

Marc nodded, his expression serious as he turned to face Nicholas. 'I know. It's just... so much has happened, and I'm not even sure where to start. And if you are up for it.'

Nicholas reached out and took Marc's hand. 'We'll start at the beginning, then. Why did you leave Ohio? What was going through your mind when you made that decision?'

Marc sighed, his gaze dropping to their joined hands. 'It wasn't just one thing. It was a culmination of so many emotions and doubts. I felt like I was caught in the middle, torn between you and Brooke. And I couldn't bear the thought of causing more pain to either of you. And her coming to the library, calling me all those names.'

Nicholas gazed with his own turmoil evident in his eyes. 'I understand how difficult that must have been. But I wish you had talked to me, told me what you felt. Maybe we could have found a way to navigate this together. You hurt me!'

Marc looked up, his gaze meeting Nicholas' with a mix of regret and longing. 'I know, I know, and I'm sorry for not being more open with you. I just... I needed time to figure things out on my own.' And tears began to stream down his face.

Nicholas took a deep breath, his grip on Marc's hand tightening. 'And what have you figured out, Marc? Do you still love me? Can we find a way to make this work?'

Marc's voice quivered as he replied, 'I hope we can because I do love you. That hasn't changed. But I'm scared, too. Scared of making the wrong decision.'

Nicholas leaned in closer, their foreheads touching as he whispered, 'We're both scared, Marc. But we won't find answers if we keep running away from this. We have to face it head-on, together. And that is me saying this. The one who has been in bed for days.'

Tears continued to well up in Marc's eyes as he nodded, a mixture of fear and hope in his heart. 'Okay, I want to try. But we need to talk to Brooke. We owe her that.'

Nicholas smiled gently, his fingers tracing Marc's cheek. 'I agree. We'll face this together. And maybe, just maybe, we can find a way to rebuild what's been broken.'

As they sat there, they held each other with small smiles and soft kisses to solidify new beginnings.

Chapter 24

Life Is Re-Opened

After a few days, Nicholas awoke to the gentle stream of sunlight that poured into Marc's bedroom. He had spent the past few days at Marc's apartment, and his spirits were gradually on the mend. Today marked his return to work, a return to the routines of his life that the whirlwind of life-changing events had disrupted.

As he lay there, he gazed at Marc, who still peacefully asleep beside him. Marc's blond hair framed his handsome face, and Nicholas couldn't help but feel a surge of affection. It was incredible how much had changed in a year, how the unexpected had weaved its way into his life.

A year ago, he would never have imagined that he'd be lying in bed beside this man. A man he had grown to love in ways he hadn't anticipated, a love that had taken him by surprise and changed the course of his life. The thought of losing Marc had been a devastating blow, one that had left Nicholas adrift and struggling to find his footing.

Now, as he watched Marc sleep, Nicholas felt a sense of gratitude wash over him. The past few days had given them a chance to reconnect, to heal some of the wounds that had torn them apart. It was a second chance, an opportunity to build something new from the ashes of their past.

With a soft smile, Nicholas leaned in and pressed a gentle kiss to Marc's forehead, silently thanking fate for bringing them back together. As they prepared to face the day ahead, he couldn't help but wonder what the future held for them, but he was determined to embrace it with an open heart and a newfound sense of hope.

As Nicholas planted a tender kiss on Marc's forehead, the warmth of the morning sunlight began to rouse Marc from his slumber. His eyelids fluttered open, revealing a pair of drowsy, yet vibrant blue eyes that met Nicholas' gaze.

'Good morning,' Nicholas whispered with a soft smile.

Marc yawned and stretched his arms above his head, his muscles flexing gracefully beneath his skin. He couldn't help but return the smile, his heart fluttering with affection. 'Morning,' he replied, his voice husky with sleep.

The two of them lay there for a moment, simply basking in each other's presence. The air felt charged with a newfound sense of possibility, a promise of what their future together might hold.

Nicholas broke the silence, his voice filled with sincerity. 'I have to go back to work today.'

Marc nodded, his fingers lightly tracing patterns on the sheet beneath them. 'Yeah, me too.'

Their return to work was a reminder of the responsibilities and commitments that awaited them in the outside world. But it was also a chance to move forward, to rebuild their lives with the lessons they had learned from their past mistakes.

Nicholas leaned in and pressed a lingering kiss to Marc's lips, a silent reassurance of the bond that had brought them back together. 'I'm glad you're here,' he murmured.

Marc met his gaze, his eyes reflecting the depth of his emotions. 'Me too,' he whispered. 'I love you, Nicholas.' The words hung in the air, heavy with meaning and the promise of a fresh start.

In a fleeting thought, Nicholas' reminder of the dinner with Brooke added a touch of complexity to their otherwise hopeful morning. Marc nodded, a mix of apprehension and determination in his eyes.

'Yeah, I remember,' he replied, shifting slightly to sit up in bed. 'It's time we have that conversation, isn't it?'

Nicholas sighed, running a hand through his hair. 'Yes, it is. I know it won't be easy, but it's something we need to do.'

Marc swung his legs over the edge of the bed and sat there for a moment, lost in thought. The prospect of facing Brooke again was daunting. He couldn't help but wonder how she truly felt about their reconciliation and what she expected from their future interactions.

'I just hope it won't turn into a heated debate,' Marc said, his brow furrowing. 'I mean, we all have issues in the drama of our lives.'

Nicholas reached out and gently squeezed Marc's shoulder. 'I hope so too, but we can't control how she reacts, and she has been great the past few days. What matters is that we stay true to our intentions and be as honest as we can.'

Marc smiled, but there was some uncertainty. Brooke had been great, but now that she can see them together, would it change? Not to mention that they were still married, he thought to himself, but he voiced, 'I know. I just... I want this to be a step toward healing, not reopening old wounds.'

Their determination to navigate the upcoming dinner with respect and understanding hung between them, but they were indifferent. There was a sense of togetherness, but Marc was still hesitant, the outsider.

As they began to prepare for the day, the promise of a fresh start, however complicated it might be, they were now in it together!

They both rose for the day. After their shower, Nicholas and

Marc chatted about the day to come. Nicholas opted for a simple, dark suit, his way of projecting confidence even though he was uncertain about the return to work after his absence. Marc, on the other hand, chose a more casual yet stylish outfit, a reflection of his desire to keep things relaxed and open.

As they made their way to the kitchen, the aroma of freshly brewed coffee filled the air—a comforting and familiar scent that provided a small measure of reassurance, a reminder to Marc of his comforting chats with his mom.

They sat across from each other at the kitchen island, both picking at their food, their thoughts still lingering. Finally, Nicholas broke the silence, his voice tinged with nervousness.

'Marc, I know we're about to face a lot of uncertainty today, but I just want you to know that I am truly happy that I am here with you,' he said, his eyes locked onto his.

Marc gave a small smile, reaching across the island to touch Nicholas' hand.

'Nicholas, we're in this together, right? We got this.'

Their fingers intertwined for a moment, a silent affirmation of their commitment to facing the evening ahead as a united front. With a shared sense of resolve, they finished their breakfast and shared a gentle kiss, the air between Nicholas and Marc seemed to lighten. It was as if that brief moment of intimacy had washed away some of the apprehension and uncertainty that had been hanging over them.

With a newfound sense of reassurance, they both grabbed their bags and headed toward the door, ready to face the day. Nicholas couldn't help but steal another glance at Marc, his heart warmed by the sight of the man he loved walking beside him.

The city outside was bustling with its usual energy, but today, it felt different. It felt like a fresh start, a chance to set things right. They hailed a cab together and climbed inside, their fingers subtly intertwined as they made their way to work.

As the cab stop near their café, Nicholas and Marc exchanged a final glance, a silent affirmation of their unity. They had faced challenges before and were determined to face this one together, no matter what it brought. With that unspoken promise, they stepped out of the cab and headed off in opposite directions.

Marc walked into the library with purpose, his steps echoing softly on the polished marble floor. The familiar scent of books and the hushed murmur of colleagues greeted him as he made his way to his desk. His return to work had been a quiet affair, with only a few colleagues aware of the circumstances surrounding his absence.

As he settled into his chair, his colleagues greeted him warmly. 'Welcome back, Marc,' one of them said with a smile, while another offered a sympathetic nod. They knew he had been struggling, and their support meant a lot to him.

Marc exchanged pleasantries with his coworkers, catching up on the latest library gossip and sharing a few anecdotes from his recent trip to Ohio. He tried to keep the conversation light, not wanting to delve into the complexities of his personal life just yet.

Despite the warm reception, his thoughts drifted to Nicholas, and the sense a of love that he felt, the love that he had… but oh… damn it… Brooke. *Why did he care?* He thought to himself, he couldn't help but feel a mixture of anxiety and hope.

As he settled into his work, organizing shelves and assisting patrons, Marc couldn't shake the feeling that his life was still on the end of the cliff. Was there still a trust issue? His head was still a whirlwind of emotion. The decisions he would make today would profoundly impact his future, and he was acutely aware of the weight of that responsibility.

Chapter 25

Lovers, Wives, or Ex's

The warm afternoon sun streamed through the café's large windows, casting dappled light patterns on the cozy tables. Nicholas sat in the corner booth, his eyes scanning the entrance every time the bell above the door chimed. His heart raced with anticipation, and he couldn't help but feel a rush of nerves.

Minutes felt like hours, and his thoughts swirled with memories of their first meeting in this very café. It was a place that held the beginning of their journey together, and today, it was the setting for a significant moment in their story.

Then, like a scene from a movie, he saw him. Marc walked in with a confident stride, his blond hair framing his elegant face. He moved past Nicholas, seemingly unaware, and disappeared around a corner. Nicholas watched him, a mix of emotions surging within him. It was as if time had both stood still and sped up all at once.

Moments later, he felt a tap on his shoulder, and he turned to see Marc standing there, a hopeful smile on his face. 'Excuse me... is this seat taken?' Marc inquired.

Nicholas couldn't help but break into a radiant smile. His eyes sparkled with emotion as he replied, 'Oh my... I love you.'

As Nicholas' fingers interlocked with Marc's, Marc couldn't help but inject a hint of sarcasm into the moment. He gave Nicholas a playful side-eye and quipped, 'Well, well, Nicholas, I must say your timing is impeccable. You finally decided to join the party.'

Nicholas chuckled, his eyes dancing with amusement. 'You know me, always fashionably late to life-changing meetings.'

Their banter brought a welcome dose of levity to the situation. They both understood the gravity of what lay ahead, but they also knew that humor had been an essential part of their connection from the beginning.

Nicholas leaned in closer, his voice softening as he spoke. 'But in all seriousness, Marc, I want you to know how much I appreciate you.'

Marc's teasing facade melted away, revealing the genuine affection he felt for Nicholas. He squeezed Nicholas' hand affectionately. 'I wouldn't be anywhere else, my dear. We're in this together, no matter what.'

Their fingers remained intertwined, a symbol of their unwavering bond, as they braced themselves for the inevitable conversation with Brooke.

As Marc and Nicholas finished their coffees, they exchanged a sweet, lingering kiss, a silent affirmation of their love and unity. They left the café, hand in hand, ready to face the inevitable meeting with Brooke. Their steps were light, their bond unbreakable, and as they turned the corner, they were met with an unexpected encounter.

Nathan, Brooke's cousin, stood there, his expression a mix of surprise and disbelief. He muttered under his breath, 'You've got to be kidding me.'

Nicholas stopped in his tracks, his grip on Marc's hand tightening briefly before he took a deep breath and turned to face Nathan. 'Nathan, not now,' he said firmly. 'Brooke and I are sorting things out, and it's none of your business.'

Marc, too, chimed in, his voice laced with a touch of irritation. 'We're just trying to move forward. We don't need any interference.'

Nathan glanced between the two of them, clearly conflicted, but eventually nodded. 'All right, fine. But you better treat her right, the both of you.'

Nicholas gave a curt nod. 'That's the plan, Nathan. Now, if you'll excuse us.'

With that, Marc and Nicholas continued down the street, their hands still intertwined, ready to face the nights challenges, both within and outside the circle of their complicated relationships.

As they walked away from the unexpected encounter with Nathan, Marc and Nicholas exchanged a wry look. It was a glance filled with relief, a shared sense of release, and a feeling of having conquered a potential obstacle in their path. They both knew that their journey was far from over, but in that moment, they felt united and ready to face whatever challenges lay ahead.

Nicholas turned to Marc, a sly smile playing on his lips. 'Well, that was an unexpected twist in our love story.'

Marc couldn't help but chuckle, his eyes reflecting a mixture of amusement and affection. 'You could say that. It seems our little drama has a knack for surprise guest appearances.'

Nicholas nodded, squeezing Marc's hand. 'True, but at least we're the main characters in this story, and we get to write our own ending.'

They made their way to Nicholas' apartment, Nicholas buzzes to let Brooke know that they are there. And they ascend the elevator.

Nicholas and Marc stood in the foyer of Marc's apartment, their fingers entwined. The atmosphere was thick with anticipation and unresolved tension. They exchanged a glance, silently affirming their solidarity as they faced whatever was to come.

From the kitchen, Brooke's voice called out with a forced cheerfulness, 'Hey, guys! I'll be right out. There is wine on the coffee table.'

As they settled into their seats in the living room, Nicholas found himself nervously tapping his fingers against the wineglass he held. He couldn't help but glance momentarily at Marc, whose face was the picture of calm and reassurance. Marc's lips curled into a playful half-smile as he felt Nicholas' tension.

'You know,' Marc quipped, his voice laced with sarcasm, 'I've heard that tapping your fingers on a wineglass is the secret code for "Let's have a serious conversation about our complicated love triangle."'

Nicholas laughed. The tension momentarily broken by Marc's humor. 'Is that right?' he replied with a teasing glint in his eye. 'And what's the secret code for "Let's make this conversation as painless as possible?"'

Brooke, who had been quietly observing the exchange, interjected with a wry smile of her own. 'I believe that code involves wine, more wine, and maybe a dash of what the fuck!'

The three of them shared a brief, genuine laugh, their nerves momentarily pushed aside. It was a small but significant step in addressing the complexities of their situation. With their glasses filled and their hearts just a bit lighter, they were ready to begin their challenging conversation about the past, the present, and the uncertain future that lay ahead.

'Here we go,' she said, pouring wine into each glass. 'Let's start by raising a toast.' She held up her glass, and the others followed suit.

'To new beginnings,' Brooke proposed, her voice steadier now.

'To new beginnings,' Nicholas and Marc echoed in unison.

They clinked their glasses, and as they took their first sips of wine, the weight of their circumstances hung in the room. The liquid did little to ease the tension, but it was a necessary lubricant for the conversation that awaited them. The atmosphere was heavy with unspoken words, regrets, and a fragile hope for resolution.

Brooke placed her glass back on the table and cleared her throat. 'I suppose we should start by addressing the elephant in the room,' she began, her voice now more somber. 'I know this situation is complicated, and there has been a lot of pain. But I believe we owe it to ourselves to have an open and honest conversation.'

Marc couldn't resist. 'Oh, come on, Brooke,' he quipped with a playful glint in his eye. 'We've already crossed so many lines and shared way too much. Why don't we just get drunk and hash it all out? We've got wine, after all.'

To Marc's surprise, Brooke chuckled at his suggestion, and Nicholas joined in. Laughter filled the room, breaking the tension even further. It was as if they were shedding the weight of their past mistakes and hurt, and in that moment, they found a glimmer of camaraderie amid the chaos.

'All right, let's do it,' Brooke agreed with a smile, pouring more wine into their glasses. 'To honesty, even when it's messy and complicated.'

They clinked their glasses together, each of them realizing that this conversation was a step toward resolving the tangled mess they found themselves in. With wine and humor as their companions, they were ready to face the truth, however painful it might be.

Brooke started, her words measured and sincere. 'I will be

honest, guys. I was angry, hurt, and confused when I found out about the two of you... a little insane. I felt betrayed, belittled, and like I'd been tossed aside.'

Marc and Nicholas exchanged a glance, their expressions a mix of empathy and regret. They knew they had caused Brooke immense pain, and there was no escaping the consequences.

'But,' Brooke continued, 'before I went to Ohio, I made a decision, and I called your mom, Marc.'

Marc's eyes widened in surprise. 'My mom? Why?'

Brooke took a deep breath. 'I needed perspective. I needed to understand why you left, why you got involved with Nick and why he was in such a state.'

'And by the way you look great,' she expressed.

Nicholas smiled, and Marc squeezed his hand.

'Jane, she's an incredible woman, and she helped me see things differently,' she continued.

Nicholas interrupted; his voice tinged with concern. 'What? Boundaries, Brooke!'

Brooke's gaze shifted between the two men. 'Boundaries? Really?' Brooke said dismissively.

'Anyway, she told me about you. About how you've always been a kind and compassionate person. And she made me realize that maybe what had happened was out of my control. She said you deserved happiness and wanted that for you.'

Marc looked touched by his mom's words but still apprehensive about where this was heading. 'Brooke, I appreciate that, but...'

Brooke held up a hand to stop him. 'Let me finish. She also made me see something about myself. She made me realize that I was clinging to something that no longer existed. That maybe it's time for all of us to consider what we truly want.'

Brooke's admission about Jane's influence in her decision to come to Ohio hung in the air. Marc looked at her, a mixture of surprise and curiosity in his eyes. 'Mom convinced you to go?' he asked, seeking clarification.

Brooke nodded, her gaze steady. 'Yes, she did. She told me that she had talked to you, and that you were struggling with your feelings and choices. She made me realize that there might be a chance to find a way through this mess, to heal and move forward.'

Marc was taken aback by his mom's involvement, but he couldn't deny the impact of her words. 'I didn't expect that,' he admitted. Marc couldn't help but smirk, 'Ah, the conniving mother of mine, always working her magic behind the scenes.'

Brooke laughed, a glimmer in her eyes. 'Yes, she did. And I think she's right. We can't change the past, Marc, but maybe, as you can see, we are here, and I think the three of us can find a way forward.'

Nicholas looked at Brooke, his gratitude evident in his eyes. 'Brooke, I don't know what to say... but thank you,' he murmured sincerely, his voice tinged with a mix of emotions.

Brooke met his gaze, her expression softening. 'Nick, I may have hated you at first, and I'm still angry with you, to be honest. But I'm trying to get past that,' she admitted, her voice carrying a trace of vulnerability. 'I realized that holding onto anger and resentment won't make any of us happy. We've all made mistakes here, and we're all hurting in some way.'

Marc, who had been listening quietly, finally spoke up, 'Brooke, I'm so sorry. I know I hurt you deeply, and I regret that. You have turned out to be such an amazing person. We can't change the past, but we can work toward a better future.'

Brooke nodded, her eyes welling up with tears. 'I appreciate your honesty, both of you,' she said, her voice trembling. 'And I'm willing to try to move forward, even if it's one step at a time.'

Nicholas and Marc, their hearts brimming with a mixture of joy, relief, and the weight of past betrayals, couldn't contain their emotions any longer. In unison, they jumped to their feet, reaching out to Brooke as if she were a lifeline. They enveloped her in the tightest, warmest bear hug they could muster.

Laughter and tears mingled in that moment, a release of pent-up emotions that had been building for nearly a year. Their intertwined bodies swayed slightly as they held onto each other, as if they were a lifeline in the turbulent sea of their past. It was a cathartic moment, a symbol of forgiveness and a commitment to a new beginning.

As they finally broke the hug, their faces were flushed, but their eyes shone with hope. It was as if a heavy burden had been lifted from their shoulders, and they were ready to take the first steps toward the future.

Chapter 26

Love and Sunshine

Nearly four years had passed since the tumultuous events that had reshaped their lives. On this warm summer day, the garden at Jane's house in Ohio was abuzz with life and joy. The scene was set for a new beginning, a fresh chapter in their intertwined stories.

The garden was adorned for a special occasion, and everyone was dressed in their finest formal attire. Brooke sat gracefully, her radiant smile matching the handsome man named Oliver beside her. It was clear that time had brought her happiness and a new love.

Across from them, under the comforting shade of a large tree, sat Marc and Jane.

Marc smiled warmly at Jane, the dappled sunlight filtering through the leaves, casting playful shadows across their faces. 'You know, Mom,' he began, 'I never would have made it through all this without your support.'

Jane's eyes shimmered with pride as she looked at her son. 'Marc, I've watched you grow, face your demons, and become the remarkable person you are today. You've come so far, and I couldn't be prouder.'

Touched by her words, Marc reached over and gently squeezed her hand. 'Thanks, Mom. You've always been my rock, and I'm grateful for everything you've done for me.'

Nicholas, on the other hand, found himself seated in the garden with a young child, Kyle, who bore a striking resemblance to him. Nicholas had embraced his role as a father with enthusiasm and love, cherishing each moment he spent with his son.

This day was not just any ordinary day, it was a day of celebration and union. It was the day of their marriage—a testament to love's resilience, forgiveness, and the capacity to evolve. Life had moved forward, and with it, the promise of extended family, enduring love, and the hope of a brighter future.

As the sun painted the sky with hues of orange and pink, the guests began to gather in anticipation of the ceremony. The garden had been transformed into a sanctuary of love, with vibrant flowers and delicate decorations adorning every corner. It was a day to remember, not just for the couple at the center of it all, but for all those who had witnessed their journey.

Marc, dressed in a sharp white suit, stood near the altar, his eyes fixed on the garden's entrance. He couldn't help but feel a rush of emotions as he thought about the path that had brought him here. It had been a journey filled with challenges, heartache, and growth. But through it all, one thing had remained constant—the deep and enduring love he felt for Nicholas.

Jane, resplendent in a flowing dress that seemed to capture the essence of summer, stood beside Marc. Her eyes shone with a mixture of pride and happiness as she watched her son prepare to exchange vows. She had played a pivotal role in bringing them all together, and today was a testament to the strength of their bonds.

Next to Jane stood Sam, he too was there to support Marc in this day of celebration. Sam looked over to see Felipe sitting next to Oliver. Brooke, too, had found her happiness. Her connection with Oliver was evident in the way they looked at each other—with admiration, respect, and a shared sense of purpose. She had come a long way from the heartbreak of the past, and the smile on her face reflected her newfound contentment.

Nicholas, holding Kyle's hand, made his way down the garden path. He was dressed in a crisp black suit, a symbol of new beginnings. His heart swelled with a mixture of nervousness and excitement. This was the day he had never thought possible—the day he would officially become Marc's husband.

As Nicholas reached the altar, he and Marc exchanged a loving and slightly nervous glance. Their journey had been far from conventional, but it had been uniquely theirs. They had weathered storms and emerged stronger, and today was a testament to their unwavering commitment to each other.

Brooke stood gracefully and joined Marc and Jane at the altar. The garden, bathed in the warm hues of the setting sun, seemed to embrace them as they prepared for the unique ceremony. Brooke, now both a witness and the officiator of their marriage, looked at the couple before her with a knowing smile.

'Dearly beloved, we gather here today to celebrate a love story that has defied convention, navigated through challenges, and emerged stronger than ever,' Brooke began, her voice carrying a sense of warmth and wisdom. She knew better than anyone the intricacies of their journey, having been a part of it herself.

'As we stand in this garden, surrounded by the beauty of nature and the warmth of your loved ones, we bear witness to a love that has endured,' Brooke continued, her words weaving a narrative of resilience and commitment. 'Love, in its truest form, is not always linear or predictable. It can be messy, complicated, and sometimes even painful. But it is also beautiful, transformative, and, above all, forgiving.'

Brooke's gaze shifted between Marc and Nicholas, they had faced such trials and tribulations and had come out on the other side with a deeper understanding of themselves and each other.

'Marc and Nicholas,' Brooke addressed them directly, 'your love story is a testament to the power of forgiveness, growth, and second chances. It reminds us that love has the ability to heal, to rebuild, and to transcend the mistakes of the past.'

She then turned to their son, Kyle, who stood beside Nicholas. 'Kyle, you are a symbol of the love that has blossomed between your fathers. You are a reminder that love knows no bounds and that family is built on a foundation of love and acceptance.'

As Brooke spoke, the sun dipped below the horizon, casting a warm, golden glow over the gathering. The atmosphere was filled with a profound sense of love and unity, as if the very garden itself was rejoicing in their union.

'Today, we celebrate not only the love that Marc and Nicholas share but also the love that has grown within this extended family,' Brooke continued. 'We celebrate the support, understanding, and the unwavering commitment to each other's happiness. And, most importantly, we celebrate the journey that has brought you to this moment.'

Brooke's words hung in the air, resonating with the hearts of all those present. She had captured the essence of their love story—the complexities, the challenges, and the profound connection that had endured it all.

'As we move forward from this day, let us remember that love is not the absence of mistakes, but the ability to learn, grow, and love even more deeply because of them,' Brooke concluded. 'Marc and Nicholas, may your love continue to flourish, your family thrive, and your journey together be filled with joy, understanding, and an unbreakable bond. Nicholas, do you take Marc to be your forever partner and husband?'

'Yes, I promise to stand by your side, to support you in all that you do, and to love you unconditionally,' Nicholas said, his voice filled with sincerity. 'I promise to be your partner, your confidant, and your best friend. I promise to cherish each day with you, for you are my heart and my home.'

'Marc, do you take Nicholas to be your forever partner and husband?'

Marc, his voice equally tender, replied, 'Yes, I promise to be there for you in times of joy and times of sorrow. I promise to listen, to understand, and to always be honest with you. I promise to love you fiercely and to be the best husband I can be. With you, I have found my truest self, and I am forever grateful.'

As they exchanged rings, the symbol of their commitment, their smiles lit up the garden. The moment they had waited for, the moment that had seemed impossible not too long ago, was finally here.

With the pronouncement of their union, cheers erupted from their loved ones. The garden seemed to come alive with joy and celebration. Kyle ran toward them, and they enveloped him in a tight embrace. They were now a family in every sense of the word.

The reception that followed was filled with laughter, heartfelt toasts, and dancing under the starry sky. It was a night to remember, a night where the past was honored, the present celebrated, and the future embraced.

The evening breeze rustled through the garden as Marc and Nicholas took to the makeshift dance floor. The soft strains of their chosen song filled the air, and they moved together, their eyes locked in an intimate gaze that spoke of the years they had spent learning each other's rhythms.

As they swayed to the music, Marc's voice was barely above a whisper. 'I can't believe we're here, dancing together like this.'

Nicholas smiled, his eyes shining with emotion. 'It's a dream come true.'

Their dance was a testament to the love that had carried them through the storm, a love that had emerged stronger and more resilient on the other side.

Meanwhile, Brooke, resplendent in her elegant dress, took a step closer to Kyle. She extended her hand, her eyes filled with warmth and affection. 'May I have this dance, young man?'

Kyle's eyes widened in surprise, and then a bright smile spread across his face. He took Brooke's hand and joined her on the dance floor. They moved together gracefully, a picture of joy and connection.

Brooke couldn't help but feel a sense of pride as she danced with the young boy who had become an integral part of her life. 'You know,' she began, 'you are lucky to have two amazing fathers who love you more than anything in the world.'

Kyle smiled, his gaze shifting between Marc and Nicholas as they danced. 'I know,' he said softly. 'And I love them too, and you Aunty Brooke.'

As the song continued, Brooke couldn't resist the urge to bring Marc and Nicholas into the dance. She approached them, and they exchanged smiles of gratitude as they welcomed her into their embrace. The four danced together in a bond of love and shared experiences.

Marc spoke as they moved gracefully across the floor. 'Brooke, we wouldn't be here without you. You played a crucial role in bringing us back together.'

Brooke's eyes shimmered with emotion. 'I just wanted to see the two of you happy again. I'm glad it all worked out.'

Their dance was a celebration of the unbreakable bond that had formed between them, a bond that had weathered the storms of the past and emerged stronger than ever. As they moved in harmony, they knew that their unconventional love story had found its own unique happily ever after.

As the evening wore on, Nicholas found himself sitting and watching his family, his loved ones. He looked at his husband, who was dancing with their son, and felt a sense of peace and contentment he had never known before.

Marc, noticing Nicholas' gaze, walked over and sat beside him. 'What an amazing day,' he stated, a soft smile on his face.

Nicholas nodded, his eyes filled with love. 'I never could have imagined that we would be here today. But I'm grateful for every twist and turn that brought us together.'

Marc placed a gentle kiss on Nicholas' lips. 'I love you more than words can express,' he whispered.

As they sat there, hand in hand, under the starlit sky, they knew that their journey was far from over. But they were ready to face whatever lay ahead, together, as they had always been—bound by love, strengthened by forgiveness, and filled with hope for the future.